WON'T STAY DEAD

STEPHEN TAYLOR

Copyright © 2019 Stephen Taylor

All rights reserved.

COVER DESIGN BY
DISSECT DESIGNS
WWW.DISSECTDESIGNS.COM

www.dissectdesigns.com

AUTHORS NEWSLETTER

For news, deals and updates why not pop over to
www.stephentaylorbooks.com and sign up for my
newsletter

ALSO BY STEPHEN TAYLOR

THE DANNY PEARSON THRILLER SERIES

Snipe

Heavy Traffic

The Timekeepers Box

The Book Signing

Vodka Over London Ice

Execution Of Faith

Who Holds The Power

Alive Until I Die

Sport of Kings

Blood Runs Deep

Command To Kill

No Upper Limit

Leave Nothing To Chance

Won't Stay Dead

Till Death Do Us Part

ALSO BY STEPHEN TAYLOR

THE DANNY PEARSON THRILLER SERIES

Sniper

Enemy Unknown

The Timekeepers Box

The Book Binding

Stolen Or London Life

Execution Of Truth

Who Holds The Power

New Dead Line

Point Of Return

Blood Runs Deep

Compared To Kill

Not Your Land

Leave Nothing To Chance

Many Stay Dead

Till Death Do Us Part

WON'T STAY DEAD

Stephen Taylor

CHAPTER 1

Afghanistan, First Tour of Duty

'Here you go, mate, get that down you,' the soldier opposite Danny said, pulling a bottle of water out of the plastic-wrapped stack and passing him one.

'Thanks, what's your name?'

'Nicholas Snipe, but everyone just calls me Snipe.'

'Daniel Pearson, everyone calls me Danny,' he replied, raising his bottle to the big soldier sitting opposite him.

A wide grin came back at him as Snipe raised his bottle back, showing off a large muscular bicep straining under his fatigues. Sweat rolled down from the blond crewcut hidden under his helmet, trickling its way past his piercing blue eyes to collect and drip off his chin. The temperature was over forty degrees in the back of the armoured Cougar Ridgeback, and the air was full of dust and grit as it carried the eight British Army soldiers through Helmand Province on their way back to Camp Bastion. It rocked and bounced across the potholes in the dirt road as they moved

1

through the centre of a remote Afghan village. Up ahead of them an armoured Jackal led the way, with a soldier manning its 50-calibre, heavy machine gun up top.

The soldiers glanced periodically out of the small, thick armoured glass windows of the Ridgeback, giving them tiny snippets of the beige-on-beige buildings outside. There wasn't much to do other than sit uncomfortably and sweat as they bounced around in the confined space, throwing banter at each other to break the odd mix of monotony and tension that came with the territory.

Danny was just draining the last of his bottle of water when the explosion went off. Eight hands grabbed the eight SA80 rifles resting between their legs, all soldiers twisting around to get a look out the small windows. The leading armoured Jackal had hit a huge IED, ripping it open and flipping it on its side. After being thrown out the top, the gunner lay in the dirt beside the Ridgeback, injured by shrapnel but alive. The driver was no more than blood stains and a pile of body parts strewn across the dirt road.

'Disembark and secure the area. Campbell, Brent, get that gunner into the Ridgeback while I call a medevac in,' came the lieutenant's voice over their earpieces as he hopped down onto the dirt road from the Ridgeback's front passenger door.

Moss jumped up onto the metal platform in the centre of the Ridgeback, pushing the top part of his body through to man the gun placement on the top. Danny and the others exited the back and took cover between the Ridgeback and a wall on the opposite side to the injured gunner, their rifles up and eyes searching the buildings opposite for hostiles.

'I've got a bad feeling about this,' Danny said, looking up at the open windows of surrounding buildings while the two medics moved into the open to retrieve the injured gunner from the destroyed Jackal. The village was eerily quiet after the noise of the IED explosion, putting their nerves on edge. Sudden gunfire and return fire broke the tension. Danny whipped his head around the back of the Ridgeback to see what was going on. A Taliban soldier wearing a camouflage jacket over his long robes flew backwards into a room in a building across the street as Moss hit him in the chest from the gun on top of the Ridgeback.

'West, how long until air support?' said the lieutenant over his headset.

'ETA twenty minutes, sir; they're coming from another skirmish sixty miles south of here,' came Todd West's response from the radio inside the Ridgeback.

Danny and Snipe darted around the back of the Ridgeback and helped the medics, Campbell and Brent, get the injured gunner inside before moving back behind the vehicle, out from the line of sight of the buildings opposite.

'Ok, listen up. Air support is twenty minutes away. Let's keep it tight. Stay behind cover and keep your eyes o—'

The lieutenant never finished his sentence. A single shot rang out from somewhere amongst the many buildings, the bullet striking the lieutenant through his left eye, killing him instantly.

'Sniper, sniper, take cover, the lieutenant's d—'

A second shot hit the gunner in his body armour before deflecting off into his shoulder, the impact causing him to fall back down inside the Ridgeback.

'Moss, you alright, Moss?' Danny called, moving with Snipe back behind the Ridgeback.

'Argh, yes, Sarge, just a flesh wound to the shoulder.'

'How's the lieutenant?' Danny said, looking to the front of the vehicle at Private Pratt.

He took his fingers off the lieutenant's neck and shook his head, knowing he was dead from the bullet wound but trying for a pulse anyway.

'West, get on to command. Tell them the lieutenant's down and we're under attack,' said Danny, knowing he was the highest-ranking officer and now in command.

'Yes, Sarge.'

Another shot rang out and ricocheted off the top of the Ridgeback, thudding into the wall behind them.

'I see the rag-headed bastard,' growled Snipe.

'Where?' Danny said.

'Between the two buildings opposite. Three-storey house set back fifty, sixty metres, top window.'

As Danny looked through his rifle sights, he caught sight of a muzzle poking out between the curtains as they flapped in the breeze. The corner of the curtain curled inward for just a second to expose the black head- and face-covering of a sniper as he lay on the floor, aiming back at them. Danny flinched away as a tiny flash emitted from the muzzle. The bullet whizzed past his ear, so close that he could feel the displaced air as it passed.

'Fuck,' he said as Snipe ducked down beside him.

'Bastard's got us pinned down. He'll have half a dozen of his mates here in a jiffy if we don't do something about it.'

Danny looked over at him and nodded.

'Pratt, you, West and Campbell give me and Snipe covering fire on my mark. We're going in to neutralise the sniper.'

'Yes Sarge,' came multiple voices, one after another.

'Now we're talking. I'm right behind you, Sarge,' said Snipe grinning, his eyes burning with excitement.

Danny took a quick peep around the Ridgeback at a thin alley opposite, following it with his eyes to the building containing the sniper. Another bullet ricocheted off the Ridgeback as he folded back into cover.

'On three. Short bursts, ok, keep the bastard's head down until we're in the alley. One, two, three.'

Pratt, West and Campbell popped up out of cover and fired, their bullets popping sandy puffs of render off the wall around the sniper's window, making him move away for cover inside. With bullets flying overhead, Danny and Snipe ran across the dirt road to the alley. They slid their backs against the gritty rendered wall, its colour the same as the sandy floor and roughness scuffing the back of their body armour.

The height of the buildings on either side of the alley put them in the shade and safely out of the line of sight of the sniper. They moved swiftly along to the door of the three-storey building, folding flat against the wall on either side. Danny reached across far enough to turn the door handle until it clicked open and swung back a few millimetres.

'Door's open, I'll go in and right, you cover left. On three,' Danny said, psyching himself up for a quick entry.

'Roger that,' Snipe said back, his blue eyes still burning with menace and excitement.

The look unnerved Danny a little, but he shook it off. 'One, two, three.'

Danny planted a boot into the door, catapulting it open as he brought his rifle across to cover the small, dark living room inside. It was typically bare, with rugs and cushions covering the floor. A woman and her elderly mother sat silently in one corner, their eyes showing neither fear nor alarm as Snipe moved into the room ahead of Danny. He pointed his rifle at them before ducking into the basic kitchen at the rear of the building. He reappeared a few seconds later, shaking his head. Danny held his hand up to the women and waved his palm up to stay where they were, before putting a finger to his lips for them to be quiet.

Danny and Snipe turned and looked up the stone staircase to the first floor. Easing his way up, one step at a time, Danny stopped halfway while Snipe walked up backwards behind him, the two of them covering downstairs and directly above at the same time. Just as Danny got high enough to see into the first-floor room, a Taliban soldier ran into view, his AK-47 rifle moving quickly around in Danny's direction. He screamed, 'Allahu Akbar,' firing wide as Danny tapped two bullets into centre mass, dropping him like a stone.

'Is that the sniper?' Snipe said as they entered the bedroom.

At that moment, a grenade bounced down the stairs from the second storey. Danny dived at Snipe, sending them bouncing painfully down the stairs until they lay halfway between the ground and first floors. The grenade went off in the bedroom above them, sending dust, grit, and bits of masonry raining down on them.

'Oh, this fucker is so dead,' growled Snipe, pulling himself off Danny before charging up into the bedroom.

By the time Danny got to his feet and headed up after him, Snipe had dived and twisted to land on his back at the base of the stairs to the second floor, his rifle held firmly in front of him as he sprayed the room above with bullets, cutting across the sniper's middle as he tried to move out the way.

'Snipe, wait,' Danny called after him.

Oblivious to him, Snipe was on his feet and heading up to the third floor before the screaming sniper hit the floor. A single shot rang out just before Danny reached him. When he did, the sniper was dead, gunshot wounds across his middle and a single bullet hole in the centre of his forehead.

'He went for his gun, ok,' Snipe said, kicking the dropped AK-47 so it slid across the floor next to the body, the look on Snipe's face challenging Danny to question the kill.

'Sarge, you need to get back here now. We have movement on the edge of town,' said Todd West over the radio.

'On our way,' Danny responded, turning away from Snipe to walk back downstairs.

He got to the ground floor with Snipe's footsteps not far behind him. As Danny exited the house into the alley, Snipe paused and turned back to the old woman and her daughter cowering in the lounge.

'Fucking ragheads,' he growled, his blue eyes blazing as he grinned and raised his rifle, shooting the old woman through the heart before turning to shoot the daughter in the head.

'Snipe, come in, Snipe?' Danny said over his radio as he turned back to Snipe emerging out the door.

'We missed one. He was hiding in the kitchen cupboard,' Snipe said matter-of-fact, walking past Danny towards the Ridgeback.

'What have we got?' Danny said over his throat mic.

'A couple of pickups with 50-cals mounted on the back. They came into view on the edge of town, then turned out of sight behind the houses.'

'Air support?'

Before the words left his mouth, the whomp of Merlin helicopter blades preceded its view by seconds as it flew past just above the houses. It banked hard over the edge of the town, the gunner letting rip on the vehicles and the men inside, shredding them both before turning and flying overhead to land on a clearing a hundred metres from the

Ridgeback. They drove out to meet it, unloading the dead lieutenant, the injured gunner and Moss. As soon as the helicopter lifted off the deck, they drove out of the town and headed back to Camp Bastion.

'Good work, guys,' Danny said as they clambered out of the Ridgeback back at base.

'Yeah, it was a blast,' said Snipe, chuckling as he turned to walk away.

'Snipe, Pearson. Major Fielding wants to see you ASAP.'

'Yes sir,' they said simultaneously and headed towards the major's office.

They stood to attention while the officer in the front office went through to the major to announce them.

'Pearson and Snipe for you, Major.'

'Thank you, Drake. Show them in.'

Danny and Snipe marched into the room, separated, and stood to attention in front of the major's desk.

'At ease.' He waited a second for them to comply, then carried on. 'I know you've had an extremely trying day, so I'll get straight to the point. You're being transferred, gentlemen.'

'Sir, where, sir?' Danny said.

'Back to the UK, some sort of MoD research project. So pack your stuff, gentlemen, there's a transport plane leaving for RAF Brize Norton at nineteen hundred hours. There will be someone at the other end to escort you to your posting.'

Danny and Snipe looked at each other in surprise and then back at the major, but no further information was forthcoming.

'That will be all, gentlemen,' the major said sharply.

'Sir,' both Snipe and Danny said, standing at attention and saluting before marching out of the office.

8

'What the fuck was that all about?' Danny said as they headed back to the barracks to pack.

'Good news. I reckon we've been fast-tracked for greater things, mate,' Snipe said with a smile.

A few hours later they were strapped into the seats lining the sides of the huge C17 Globemaster as it took off, leaving Afghanistan far behind.

CHAPTER 2

Project Jericho

After an uncomfortably long seven hours, the C17 Globemaster touched gently down on the tarmac at RAF Brize Norton. It taxied off the main runway, travelling to the far side of the airfield before stopping. The winding down of the engines signalled they were at their final destination. Moments later a red warning lamp illuminated and the enormous loading ramp lowered to the tarmac.

Danny and Snipe grabbed their kit bags and walked to its edge. A black Range Rover with privacy glass windows pulled up behind the aircraft as the ramp touched the ground. They walked off the plane into the cold air and stood to attention as a man in uniform climbed out of the car, the sergeant stripes on his arm marking his rank.

'At ease, men. I'm Sergeant Gary Burns. I'm here to take you to your accommodation whilst you're with us,' he said, opening the boot for them to put their kit bags in.

'Nice car, Sarge, not your usual army transport,' said Snipe with a grin.

'You're not going to your usual military facility, son. Now in you get.'

Snipe climbed into the front passenger seat while Danny got in the back. Since he'd been a small boy, Danny had always had a sixth sense about things, and as the door closed, his senses were giving him a really bad feeling about wherever they were going. After showing his ID at the gate, Sergeant Burns drove off the base, following the perimeter fence past the buildings and hangars inside, past the giant runway, until only dark fields lay ahead.

They eventually joined the A40 and headed towards London. Danny nodded off for a while, only waking when Sergeant Burns turned off the M40 just outside Uxbridge. They headed through the countryside, turning here and there, eventually slowing when they entered a dense woodland. Half a mile in, the sergeant turned off the main road and down a long tarmac driveway. He kept going for about a mile until floodlights in the distance cut beams of light through the trees, giving tiny previews of the large clearing up ahead.

The tree line fell away, and two buildings came into view behind a high chain-link fence. They looked like old barrack blocks, square, brick-built buildings with rows of uniformed windows along both sides, with a large hall attached to the back of one of them. As they moved through the open chain-link gates, armed military police moved out from a newly built security hut and stopped them by a barrier. Looking along the floodlit fence, Danny could see that they'd recently upgraded its top with great spirals of shiny razor wire. Sergeant Burns lowered his window and showed his ID and paperwork to the MPs. He lowered the rear window next to Danny so the guard could shine a torch in at Danny and then Snipe to identify them.

'Very good, sir,' he said, standing to attention while another guard raised the barrier.

They drove around to the second block and parked. After grabbing their bags, they followed the sergeant inside and up the stairs to the third floor, eventually stopping outside two rooms with their doors open.

'Get some sleep, gentlemen. The toilets and showers are at the end of the corridor. Tracksuits and trainers are in your lockers. You are to wear them unless told otherwise. There is a sports hall at the rear of this building. It doubles up as a mess hall for breakfast, lunch and dinner. Please make your way over to the research building by ten hundred hours, where there will be a briefing.' The sergeant spun on his heels and marched off, leaving them to enter their rooms.

The interior was much like Danny expected, with a single steel-framed bed with crisp cotton sheets and an itchy MoD-issue blanket. A table and lamp sat on one side of the bed, with a steel locker on the other. Deadbeat, Danny quickly unpacked his kit bag, put his things in the locker beside the provided tracksuits, and went to bed. He cleared his mind, pushing thoughts of a day that started with an IED attack and ended over three and a half thousand miles away in an old barracks building on the outskirts of London out of his mind. Closing his eyes, he breathed calmly and fell instantly asleep.

CHAPTER 3

Danny awoke in the morning as he always did, the internal clock in his head telling him to open his eyes minutes before the alarm on his phone went off. After a walk down the corridor to the showers, he dressed and made his way downstairs to the sports hall. He entered the hall equipped with weights, benches, and an assortment of running, rowing and cycling machines positioned at one end, a basketball court across the middle, and a long table at the bottom.

The other recruits sat around the table, while two cooks worked in a small kitchen behind a long steel-shuttered serving hatch. They put on a decent array of bacon, eggs, sausages, and other breakfast foods. Danny loaded up his plate and walked over to the table, taking a seat amongst seven other men, presumably newly arrived for whatever this was. Snipe sat at the head of the table, his sheer size making that the best place for him to sit, so his shoulders and elbows didn't get in anyone's way. He looked Danny's way, grinned, and winked before returning to shovelling

13

food in his mouth, the knife and fork looking like kid's cutlery in his large hands.

'Morning mate, I'm Sean,' said the guy to Danny's left.

'Danny.'

This triggered a stream of introductions around the table that turned into a general murmur of chat and army banter about what regiment and where they had all been serving before arriving at the centre.

'So, what do you reckon about all this?' Danny said to Sean.

'Fuck knows. We're probably filling some government charter somewhere. How to make us more rounded individuals, too many soldiers coming out of conflict with PTSD, that sort of bollocks.'

'Hmm, you're probably right,' Danny replied.

'Look on the bright side, the food's good and we're not getting shot at,' a young Welsh guy called Will said with a grin from across the table.

After breakfast they all left the accommodation block and headed past the mostly empty car park to the research building next door. Glancing towards the rear of the buildings, Danny could see an assault course with what looked like windowless, tactical training buildings further on. Beyond the training buildings was dense woodland, shielding the research facility from view on all sides. Brand new razor-wire-topped fencing ran along either side of the area, disappearing out of sight as it entered the woods, the metal not exposed to the elements long enough for it to dull and tarnish to an oxide grey.

'Someone has gone to a lot of trouble for a few fitness and psych tests,' thought Danny.

Sergeant Burns stood inside and guided them into a room as they entered the building. They sat down in a row of chairs and waited. The crossed baton and sabre beneath a star and crown epaulette made them all jump to attention as a general led several people into the room.

'As you were, gentlemen. I am General Neil Cracknell, and I am in charge of this research project. To my left are Lieutenant Henry Thomas and Sergeant Gary Burns. They will be running the day-to-day schedule which will involve physical and tactical exercises. To my right are Dr Heinrich Mann, Dr Samantha Mandrell and Dr Vihaan Kapur. They are experts in genetics, haematology and neuroscience. They will be running tests, taking bloods, and administering tablets and injections daily. These are a variety of vitamins and proteins to put you all on an even base line.

'The purpose of these experiments is to help us get an accurate picture of the mental and physical state of our armed servicemen and women. We have selected all of you based on your exceptional scores in basic training, performance on tour, and impeccable service records. The project will last for twelve weeks, and we expect your full cooperation during that time. If any of you do not wish to take part, this is the time to say so. You will be transferred back to your unit with immediate effect. If you decide to take part, the MoD will grant you a transfer to the regiment of your choice. Any questions?'

All eight men sat still and quiet. They were all ambitious and had all put in applications for various elite regiments. Plus, they knew that when a general wraps up his speech and asks if there are any questions, it really means: I'm done, shut up and do as you are told.

'Right. Excellent. I'll leave you in the capable hands of Lieutenant Thomas,' the general said, turning to leave the room.

'Attention!' yelled the lieutenant, making them all bolt upright and salute the general as he left the room. 'At ease.

Sergeant Burns will hand you some forms to sign. These are official non-disclosure agreements and medical waivers. Once you've signed them, Walters, Pearson and Fox, you will follow me. The rest of you take a seat until your name is called.'

CHAPTER 4

anny, Walters and Fox followed the lieutenant out into the hall and down a clinical-looking corridor to a square waiting room with numbered doors leading off it and a row of chairs in the middle.

'Sit here and wait to be called. When the doctors finish with you, take a seat out here and wait to be called again, ok?'

'Yes, lieutenant,' they said in unison.

Walters and Fox were called into rooms 022 and 023 moments before Dr Mandrell called Danny into room 024. She was a tall, skinny, black woman who addressed him with a thick South African accent.

'Please, sit down, Mr Pearson.'

'So what goes on in here?' Danny said, looking around at the multitude of machines and screens in the room.

'I'm a neuroscientist, Mr Pearson. These machines measure your brain activity while you perform a number of problem-solving tasks and reactionary tests.'

'Great, next you'll be asking me to put on one of those

silly hats and play computer games,' Danny said with a smile that made Dr Mandrell laugh a little before quickly correcting herself.

'Yes, Mr Pearson, it is silly hat time. This is an EEG cap, short for electroencephalography. It measures the brain's electrical activity while we get you to perform tasks on the computer,' she said while sliding across to him what essentially looked like a swimming cap covered with sensors connected to a loom of cables leading back to a computer.

The tests went on for about half an hour. When they were over, Dr Mandrell took the EEG cap off and took a gun-like object with an air line attached to it off the work-top. She inserted a small bottle with a yellow liquid into the top of it.

'I'm going to give you a gas injection. It's completely painless. The drug is a synthetic equivalent of the natural drug your brain produces. It's a very small dose and completely harmless. You may feel a slight rush, as if the world around you is slowing down. This is normal and will pass shortly. It is just the effect of your brain's neuron connectors communicating at an accelerated rate. This will also make your reflex actions feel like they are pre-emptive rather than reactionary.'

Danny didn't say anything. He just nodded and let her place the nozzle of the injector over the carotid artery in his neck. As soon as she pulled the trigger, it let out a sharp hiss and was done. A couple of seconds later Danny felt a rush of blood to the head, and everything in the room seemed to shout out as his brain took in a mass of informa-tion from everything in his main and peripheral vision. The rush subsided fairly quickly, but still left him feeling like he was over awake or wired on too much coffee.

'That's all. If you would like to wait outside, someone will call you to one of the other rooms.'

Danny did as she said and was pleased when Dr Kapur, the haematologist, only took a couple of vials of blood from him and sent him back into the waiting room. Finally, he was called into room 023 where the geneticist, Dr Mann greeted him and took a swab from his mouth for DNA study. When all three were finished and sitting in the waiting room, Sergeant Burns appeared and sent them back to the accommodation block, where they congregated in the sports hall.

'Fuck me, that was a rush. It feels like there's a party going on in my head. Like I can feel the room. Hey Dave, chuck me an apple,' Snipe shouted as he walked into the mess hall.

David Smith picked up an apple and lobbed it at Snipe. One of his tree trunk sized arms shot out and caught it without looking in its direction.

'You see that. I fucking felt it coming. I've gotta get me some more of that shit the pretty little South African's dishing out,' Snipe said with a chuckle.

'Yeah, well, all I've got is a splitting headache,' said Sean Walters, rubbing his forehead.

Danny sat eating lunch without saying a word, his senses tingling as he felt the room the same way Snipe did.

The rest of the afternoon was free time. Most of the lads spent it in the hall, working out or playing basketball. Shortly before lights out, the Sergeant and Dr Mann did the rounds, administering three tablets which had to be taken on the spot. The Sergeant left instructions that they were to meet on the training ground at zero eight hundred hours tomorrow.

CHAPTER 5

When Danny awoke, although still there, the effect of the injection the previous day had dulled considerably. He put on a tracksuit and met the others in the hall for breakfast. Everyone was in high spirits with the usual army piss-taking banter, apart from Sean who still complained of a splitting headache. At eight o'clock they assembled by the assault course, standing to attention, when Lieutenant Thomas and Sergeant Burns approached. The two officers immediately put them through a gruelling three hours on the assault course, timing and recording their results after each run before sending them back to the start line, time and time again.

'Right, you lot, gather round. Get showered and changed, then get some food. I want you all in the research centre hall by thirteen hundred hours.'

Eating heartily after the morning's gruelling exercise, Danny watched Sean across the table. He joined in with the banter but looked pained and rubbed his temple every few minutes.

'Your head still bothering you?' Danny asked.

'Yeah, I've got a proper thumper going on,' Sean replied with a half-hearted smile.

'Tell them to give you something. There are enough bloody doctors over there. I'm sure one of them can cure a headache,' Danny said, noticing Snipe's head turn in their direction, his intense blue eyes locking onto Sean.

'Come on, Sean, you pussy, suck it up, man. You need a brain to have a fucking headache,' he mocked with a big grin on his face.

Snipe's banter and voice sounded friendly, but Danny noticed his intense stare and body language, eager for Sean to retaliate. Sean didn't rise to the bait, he just ignored him. A few seconds later, as if flicked by a switch, Snipe's body language relaxed and he moved on, chatting with the others.

By thirteen hundred hours, they all sat in the hall and waited to be called. The afternoon went by with more tests and another injection in the neck from Dr Mandrell, followed by the same head rush as the day before. When Danny was called into Dr Kapur's room, he put an IV line into Danny's arm and hooked him up to a bag of yellowish fluid that seemed almost fluorescent. The doctor told him it was to wash toxins out of the blood and add proteins and iron to enhance the transfer of oxygen to the muscles.

Danny stifled a yawn as he waited for the bag to empty, but by the time it had, he had to admit he felt amazing, exploding with energy, like he could run a marathon with no sweat. After the doctors had seen everyone, the lieutenant sent them back to the accommodation block. They kept the boredom at bay by spending the evening in the recreation room, watching TV or playing darts and pool to pass the time, all except Sean, who, with his head still banging, went to bed early. Pool was the winner stays on, and even though Danny was last up to play, Snipe hadn't stepped off the table.

'Come on, Pearson, rack 'em up. Let's be having my next victim,' Snipe said with a gravelly chuckle.

Danny was a good player. His dad used to take him and his brother Rob down to the social club to play as kids. The difference between before the research centre's treatments and now struck him the moment he leaned forward to take his shot; his mind was clearer, sharper. The angle needed to put the ball into the pocket just popped out at him. He could feel every tiny muscle and had more control over the power as he jabbed the cue into the white for the shot.

The game started off friendly, but as Danny potted more balls, Snipe got increasingly agitated. He tried to get ahead but missed a crucial shot, leaving the game open to Danny.

'For fuck's sake, this bloody table's warped,' Snipe grumbled loudly, his arms waving about as he gestured towards the table.

The room erupted into laughter with comments of 'Fuck off, you loser,' and 'Take it like a man.' The muscles in Snipe's cheeks flexed as he gritted his teeth, his eyes blazing angrily as Danny potted the last coloured ball before moving around to the black and potting it for the win.

'Good game, mate,' Danny said to Snipe.

'Fuck off, you prick,' Snipe growled back, throwing the cue on the table before leaving the room.

'Someone's a bad loser. Here, I'm up next,' said Will in his thick Welsh accent.

'There's something not right about that guy. He scares the shit out of me,' said Aaron, retrieving his darts from the dartboard.

22

CHAPTER 6

The next morning Snipe was back to cracking jokes and bantering around the breakfast table. All were present apart from Sean. Before Danny had a chance to go and see how he was, Sergeant Burns marched into the hall.

'At ease,' he said, catching them before they could stand to attention. 'Gentlemen, I want you on the training ground in thirty minutes. Mr Walters won't be joining us. He has had to leave the program on medical grounds.'

The room fell silent until the sergeant left.

After a morning of exercises and then lunch, they all assembled in the research centre's meeting room. Lieutenant Thomas called them one by one at ten minute intervals. Eventually it was Danny's turn. He followed the lieutenant down the clinically clean corridor, turning right at the end before entering a room he hadn't been in before.

'Sit there and wait for Dr Mandrell,' the lieutenant said before leaving the room.

Danny took a seat and looked around the white-painted room. A desk sat below a viewing window opposite him and computer screens sat on top next to a chunky white metal box with switches, dials and a joystick. Danny got up and walked across, leaning on the desk to look through the viewing window. The glass was thick, maybe two or three inches, with a film embedded below its surface, giving the view of the room on the other side a greenish tinge. It was windowless, with metal panelling on all sides. A flat, padded bed sat dead centre of the room on adjustable metal arms. Two giant robotic arms stood on either side of the bed, a large sphere on the end of each one. Danny accidentally nudged the mouse on the desk as he leaned in to look closer. The monitor screen in front of him burst into life. A bunch of cross-sectioned images of the inside of someone's head appeared, with Test Subject Williams written at the top.

'Good morning, Mr Pearson,' came Dr Mandrell's voice from behind him.

'Oh, er, sorry, I was just having a look when the screen came on. What is this?'

'Just an X-ray machine, nothing to worry about.'

'Bit heavy duty for just an X-ray machine,' Danny said, tapping the glass.

'Well, if I wound it up to max, I might be able to warm my lunch in there. But don't worry, Mr Pearson, you're in safe hands, we're just taking an X-ray today. Now, shall we?' Dr Mandrell said with a smile while opening the thick metal door to the X-ray room.

Fourteen days went by and the tests, the injections, and pills continued. Physically, they all excelled, powering through the assault course and exercises with ever-increasing speed. Mentally, cracks were showing among some of the men. Aaron Jones had withdrawn into himself. He didn't join in with the banter and only talked if someone addressed him directly. James Fox was a bag of nerves, jumpy and avoiding direct eye contact, especially when Snipe displayed his ever-growing aggressive behaviour. Danny felt alive. Apart from a spate of weird dreams, his senses were in overdrive. He topped the assault course, always just ahead of Snipe, and moved through Dr Mandrell's neurology tests at lightning speed. In combat scenarios in the training buildings beyond the assault course, Danny felt like he sensed the surrounding team, stopping short of rooms to hear their breathing or feel their heartbeat from metres away.

Leaving his room, Snipe plodded down the corridor in his shorts and T-shirt. He turned into the bathroom and backed his massive frame into a cubicle to sit down and take a crap. He heard someone else enter the bathroom, followed by a tap running.

'I wouldn't come in here without a gas mask or a canary if I were you, mate, that curry's gone right through me,' Snipe called out with a chuckle.

He waited for the usual comical reply, but got none. The tap stopped running and footsteps died away.

'Alright, please, your fucking self,' he muttered to himself.

He finished up, washed his hands, and headed past the stairs towards his room. The heavy click of the door closing at the top grabbed his attention.

Hello what's going on up there then?

Snipe walked up the stairs and opened the door onto the roof. Aaron Jones stood ten metres away, lit up in the silvery glow of a full moon. His toes protruded over the edge of the building, and his body swayed slightly as he stared down at the car park below.

'Alright, Jones, me old mucker? What are you doing up here then, mate?' Snipe said.

Aaron didn't move.

25

'Oi dickhead, I asked you what you're doing,' Snipe repeated, instantly irritated.

Aaron's head came up and he turned slowly to face Snipe.

'I can't stop the noises in my head, voices mocking me, telling me to do things, terrible things, and the dreams, nightmares,' Aaron said, his eyes watery and tears trickling down his cheeks.

Snipe stood still, his intense blue eyes staring unblinkingly into Aaron's. After a minute or so a wide grin spread across Snipe's face.

'Man up, Aaron, you fucking whining prick. Do I look like your fucking mum? You want to see a nightmare, son, you look into my eyes, because I'm your worst nightmare, mate.'

Snipe took a step towards Aaron, stopping when he flinched and swayed on the building's edge.

'What, you going to jump? Go on then. Nah, you haven't got the balls for it,' Snipe said in a low, gravelly voice.

Snipe took two aggressive steps forward, making Aaron flinch and wobble. A moment of panic flashed across Aaron's face as he lost balance and dropped silently off the edge of the building into the darkness.

Snipe walked up to the edge, an excited twinkle in his eyes as he looked down at Aaron's broken body lying on the tarmac. 'Fucking lightweight,' he muttered before turning and walking away. He headed back down the stairs and along the corridor to his room.

'Oi Hurne, leave it alone, alright. I don't want to hear you wanking all night,' he bellowed as he passed David Hurne's room and turned into his own.

'Fuck off, dickhead,' Hurne yelled back.

CHAPTER 7

D anny glanced out of the window on his way downstairs for breakfast. A black panelled van and an army jeep sat outside the research centre, and two guys in army green overalls were busy jet washing the paved area in front of their accommodation block. The scene struck him as odd, but he pulled himself away and entered the hall. Midway through breakfast, Lieutenant Thomas entered and informed everyone that Aaron Jones had been withdrawn from the project on medical grounds.

'And then there were six,' Snipe said, lifting his head from his breakfast to give everyone a massive grin.

On his way back out of the hall, Danny looked back outside. The van had gone, and the men had finished jet washing and were loading the pressure washer into the back of an army jeep. A black Land Rover came through the gate and parked up by the research building. General Neil Cracknell got out to be met by Lieutenant Thomas and Dr Mann before entering the building. By their mannerisms and facial expressions, none of them were very happy. Turning back to the other soldiers coming out of breakfast behind him, Danny looked at them closely. A mixture of twitchy, pale, withdrawn faces looked back at him, and in Snipe's case, there was something a little crazy in his eyes. Something was wrong here—very wrong.

Over in the research building, the general assembled the doctors. He waited for the lieutenant to leave the room before speaking.

'Well?'

'I admit, this is a minor setback, but—' Dr Mann started to say.

'But nothing. Two dead men in two weeks is not a minor setback; it's a goddamn shitstorm. I've got Whitehall on the verge of shutting the project down,' the general barked.

'You can't, General. We have real results here. The candidates have shown massive improvement. Pearson, Snipe, and Hollander's mental processing and spatial awareness are nothing short of spectacular, as are their blood delivery systems and physical endurance.'

'Mmm, Dr Mandrell, what have you got to say?' The general said, turning his attention her way.

'It's true, General. We are seeing groundbreaking results in some candidates, but I am seeing worrying signs of depression, paranoia and psychosis in several of the others.'

The general looked at the three doctors, deep in thought.

'Get this shit under control, people. I'll keep Whitehall at bay for now. You do what you have to do, but no more fuck ups.'

Eyeing the doctors with a withering look, the general turned and left the room.

'We'll reduce the levels of treatment and monitor the

candidates. Dr Mandrell, can you increase the psychological evaluations to every other day instead of weekly?'

'Yes, Dr Mann,' Dr Mandrell said, the three of them leaving to their separate rooms in silence, the excitement and confidence of the early research results slipping away with every step.

CHAPTER 8

Ten days had gone by since the announcement that Jones had withdrawn from the program. Danny noticed the other candidates' moods had seemed to improve, although Brent and Fox still seemed withdrawn. The tests were relentless, as were the fitness drills and mission exercises. They were tolerable, but daily shrink sessions with Dr Mandrell were getting irritating. Danny couldn't take much more of the 'how are you feeling' and 'what was your relationship with your parents?' bullshit. As he sat, avoiding some of the more futile questions, his eyes wandered past Dr Mandrell to the view out across the exercise field. Movement over by the sheds where they kept the ride-on mower and groundsman's tools caught his eye. The door to the shed slid open and James Fox emerged carrying a petrol canister.

'Have you noticed any change in your mood, Mr Pearson?' Dr Mandrell said, noticing his distraction. She wheeled her chair across to block Danny's eye line and gain his focus.

'Only since these bloody sessions started,' Danny said

with a frown, leaning in the opposite direction to see Fox heading across the grass.

Fox walked over to the assault course. He moved past the balancing beam and obstacle wall, coming to a halt underneath the monkey bars.

What the fuck is he doing?

It was a fair way away, but as Fox turned to face the building, Danny could see the expression of hopelessness written on his face. He unscrewed the top of the petrol canister and chucked it on the ground.

'Mr Pearson, can we please get back to the questions?' said Dr Mandrell impatiently.

'Shit, don't do it. Call an ambulance, now!' Danny shouted, exploding out of his seat and heading out the door.

Dr Mandrell spun around in her chair to see what Danny had been looking at, and saw Fox still holding the petrol canister above himself, the highly flammable liquid splashing off his head as it flowed all over him.

'Oh god no,' she said, reaching for the phone.

By the time Danny swerved around Snipe in the corridor and charged through the doors to the outside, Fox had emptied the can, dropped it on the floor and pulled a lighter out of his pocket.

'Fox, no, don't do it!' Danny yelled, his arms and legs pumping as he ran towards him with everything he had.

There was a flash of blue as the petrol vapours ignited ahead of the liquid. A millisecond later, Fox vanished inside a ball of orange flame. He stood motionless for a second before screaming and falling to his knees. His arms flailed about, then the screaming stopped, and his arms dropped by his side. Danny was gaining ground, pulling his tracksuit top off as he ran. By the time Danny got to Fox, he'd fallen face down and wasn't moving. Danny dived on top of him while holding his top out between his hands, and frantically patted him down until he extinguished the last of the flames.

Throwing the tracksuit top aside, Danny rolled Fox onto his back. A bloody, burnt mess of flesh looked lifelessly back at him. Clinging to hope, Danny put his ear to Fox's mouth but couldn't hear any breathing. He put his palms on Fox's chest and started CPR, pumping rhythmically for a thirty count before giving mouth-to-mouth. He continued for ten minutes, his palms black and bloody from the mixture of melted tracksuit and the burnt flesh of Fox's chest. The doctors, lieutenant and sergeant congregated around him with Brent, Hollander, Hurne and Snipe.

'Danny, come on, leave him, mate. He's gone,' Hollander said.

Danny stopped. He checked one last time for a pulse, knowing there wouldn't be one, then stood up slowly, looking up at the doctors.

'What the fuck have you been doing to us? And don't give any bollocks about stimulants, proteins and vitamins,' Danny said furiously at them.

'Pearson, stand down, soldier, you're out of line,' ordered Lieutenant Thomas.

'Tell me what happened to Walters and Jones. They didn't just leave, did they?' Danny continued ignoring Lieutenant Thomas, the guilt-ridden looks on the doctors' faces telling him all he needed to know.

'That's enough. All of you get back to barracks, now,' bellowed the lieutenant, stepping in between the soldiers and the doctors, Sergeant Burns stepping in behind him.

'What happened to Walters and Jones?' Danny said again through gritted teeth.

Brent, Hollander and Hurne moved around him, all with angry, determined faces.

'Nothing happened to them. They left the program. Now get back to the accommodation block before I put you all on a charge,' the lieutenant said, stepping right up to Danny so his face was inches away from him.

'Nothing, huh? That's funny. I don't know what happened to Walters, but when Jones took a dive off the roof, he had the same look on his face as Mister Crispy over there,' Snipe said, stepping forward to join the others.

'You better call the general, Lieutenant. This project is over. We're out of here,' Danny said, pushing past him, closely followed by the others.

———

Less than an hour later, a phone rang in a small office in London's Whitehall offices.

'Yes.'

'We've had another death.'

'What, General? Who?'

'James Fox. He poured petrol all over himself and then set light to it. The others are demanding they leave the project. What should I do?'

'Hmm, the project was already on its last chance. There's no way the committee will let it continue after this. Shut it down, General.'

'And the men?'

'Give them their commissions. Let's see how they perform back in the field. We'll monitor them for now, especially Pearson and Snipe. When the time's right, we'll bring them into the program.'

'And the doctors?'

'Send them home, General. Project Jericho is over.'

There was a knock at the door as he put the phone down.

'Come.'

A small man entered, carrying a thick file.

'Good morning, Howard, I have that report you wanted on that former KGB arms dealer, Rufus Petrov.'

'Ah excellent, Trevor, thank you very much.'

CHAPTER 9

Two Years After Project Jericho

'Hey, Danny, your transfer from D-Squadron's coming in on a chinook in five minutes.'

'Ok thanks, mate,' Danny said, leaving the comms building to join the other two men in his unit standing outside.

They were all armed and in full kit, sweating in the hot Afghanistan sun.

'Cutting it a little fine, aren't we, Staff?' Smudge said to Danny.

'No choice, Smudge. Intel says this guy's a high-ranking Taliban member and will only be in the village until tonight. Ferg's out of action with a fractured collarbone, and we need four men. So we take this guy and go with it,' Danny said, walking ahead of the others to the helicopter landing area.

'Who have we got then?' Chaz asked.

'Don't know, just one of the guys from D-Squadron, that's all I know.'

They could hear the chinook approaching from the south before they saw it, a hazy black dot that rippled and shook as the hot midday thermals floated across its image, distorting their view. As it gained in size, the shape sharpened up. Two sets of rotor blades appeared through the haze, cutting circles in the air as they spun. The low whomp hit them in the chest as it grew louder, deafening them as the helicopter passed over the perimeter wall of the base before banking around to land fifty metres ahead of them. All three of them turned their heads away, their wraparound sunglasses only offering a little protection against the sand and grit blasting their way from the downdraft. The engines wound down and the rear door lowered to the ground to create a loading ramp. A huge, solid-looking soldier stepped out in full kit, his face hidden from view by shades, a helmet, and a scarf wrapped around his nose and mouth.

'Big fucker, isn't he?' said Chaz.

'Yeah, if the shooting starts, I'm standing behind him,' chuckled Smudge.

Danny stared at the man as he approached. His shape and the way he walked looked familiar. He walked straight up to Danny and reached up, pulling the scarf down to reveal a wide grin.

'Alright, me old mate, this is just like old times,' Snipe said with a big grin.

'Snipe, good to have you on board. This is Charles Leman, call him Chaz, and this is Darren Smith, Smudge.'

'Alright fellas,' Snipe turned to them to give a nod before turning back to Danny. 'Well, are we going to get on with whatever this urgent mission is, or are we going to stand here chewing the fat all day? Because I'm on a promise back at camp. Her name's Fatima, she's a lovely little number, beautiful body once you get the suicide vest off,' Snipe said, laughing loudly as he followed Danny and the others.

'Transport's this way, I'll brief you en route,' Danny said over his shoulder. He wasn't that keen on Snipe, but for all his faults, he was a damn good soldier.

They took a beaten-up old Land Cruiser from the motor pool and headed out of the camp. Smudge drove while Chaz sat beside him in the front. Danny sat in the back, briefing Snipe on the covert mission to find a Taliban general named Nasser Al-Zawahiri, capture him and return him to camp for interrogation. A local informer reported him to be in one of two properties inside a walled compound in a village twenty miles from their location. According to the intel, the general only had a handful of soldiers with him. The base command room was in constant communication as they watched the operation over a live satellite feed of the compound.

'How close are we going in this tub of crap?' Snipe said.

'One hundred metres from target. There's an abandoned building on the edge of the village. We'll park up in its animal compound and head down between these buildings, keeping out of sight until we're right next to the compound wall. HQ has eyes in the sky and will warn us of any resistance. Then it's a search of the buildings, grab this fucker if he's there, and hightail it back to base,' said Danny, folding the map and aerial shots of the compound and tucking them into the side pocket of his combat trousers.

'Piece of piss,' Snipe said with a smile.

Although the journey only took half an hour, it felt twice as long bouncing along on the bumpy, potholed dirt track road in the Land Cruiser with worn-out shock absorbers. The building matched the intel, and they parked up out of sight in the empty animal compound and headed towards the target buildings. The village was small, with no one on the street in the midday heat. They headed quickly between the buildings, squatting down out of sight by the compound wall surrounding the target properties.

'Alpha Team to base, we are at the compound. Have you got eyes on the target? Over.'

'Base to Alpha Team, we have you on visual. No eyes on target and the compound is empty apart from a female hanging out washing in the courtyard. Over.'

'Alpha Team to base, we are proceeding with the search. Over.'

'Affirmative, Alpha Team, you are good to go.'

They moved along the wall to a gate, surprised to find it unlocked. They opened it a crack before sprinting to the corner of the building. Peeping around it, they could see the woman in the courtyard hanging out sheets to dry. No one else appeared to be around or looking out any of the property's windows.

'I'll get her,' Snipe said, heading off without Danny's ok.

'Snipe,' Danny said in a whisper down the radio mic.

Moving with surprising stealth for a man of his size, Snipe crept up behind the woman and grabbed her, one hand across her mouth and the other around her waist, lifting her off the floor as he scooted backwards towards the others. He spun her around to face the others, her eyes wide in panic as she clawed at his hand, trying to get it off her mouth.

'Calm down, we're not going to hurt you,' Danny said, his tone friendly as he put a finger to his lips for her to be quiet.

He reached down and pulled the picture of Nasser Al-Zawahiri from the side pocket of his combat trousers. Holding it up in front of the woman, he tapped the photo and pointed at the first building, then the second.

'Him, is he here?' Danny didn't know if she spoke English, but his directions were clear enough.

She looked at the photo while Danny watched her closely. No sign of recognition flashed in her eyes, and she shook her head as much as she could with Snipe's massive hand and forearm around her mouth and neck.

'Shit, I don't think he's here. Smudge, you bring up the rear. Snipe, bring her inside with us. Chaz on me,' Danny said to three understanding nods.

Moving to the entrance of the first house, Danny and Chaz swept inside, peeling left and right to cover the rug- and cushion-covered lounge. An Afghan man walked into the room through the curtain of hanging beads and froze at the rifles aimed at his head. His eyes went wide when Snipe came in, pushing his wife ahead of him. He spouted a stream of Pashto at them while gesturing wildly with his hands.

'Down on the cushions, now,' Danny said, indicating for him to sit. 'Snipe, sit her down next to him and cover them. Smudge, stay by the door, cover the exit. Me and Chaz will sweep the rest of the house.'

Smudge moved just outside the door, his eyes scanning around for signs of hostiles. Danny and Chaz checked the kitchen, then disappeared upstairs to check the bedrooms.

'Hey buddy, this is your wife, yeah? Wife, eh?' Snipe said, pointing at the woman.

'Yes. Wife,' the man said in broken English.

'Nice, I bet she's a real looker under all that,' Snipe grinned. The man looked blankly back, not understanding, while his wife adjusted her headscarf to cover her face.

'Clear, target's not here,' came Danny's voice over the radio. Moments later Danny and Chaz descended the stairs. 'You and Smudge stay here and cover them while me and Chaz search next door.'

'Roger that,' said Snipe and Smudge as Danny and Chaz moved out the door and ran across to the other building.

'Now we've got a few minutes. What shall we do to pass the time?' Snipe said with menace, a big grin crossing his face as he moved closer to the man, his hand finding the handle of his commando knife.

Minutes passed. Eventually, Danny's voice came over the radio. 'Alpha Team to base, intel's bad, target is not on site. I repeat, target is not on site. Alpha Team returning to base.'

'Roger that, Alpha Team. Return to base.'

'Smudge, Snipe, leave the civilians and meet us in the courtyard. We're out of here.'

They made their way down the stairs and back outside to see Smudge moving towards them.

'Where's Snipe?'

'I don't know. He was just inside the room keeping an eye on the man and his wife,' said Smudge, looking back at the house.

'Snipe, come in,' Danny said, moving when he didn't get an answer. 'Snipe, come in.'

With rifles up, Smudge and Chaz peeled either side of the door, folding in behind Danny as he charged inside. Surprised by the noise, Snipe grabbed his rifle from a cushion and whipped around to point it at Danny. When he saw it was them, he lowered it and moved his hand up to put the radio earpiece back into his ear. Danny turned to see the man lying in a pool of blood on the floor, his throat cut. The man's wife lay motionless over the cushions, her dress pulled up around her waist, a look of terror locked on her face from the seconds before Snipe snapped her neck.

'Taliban fuckers. She had a kitchen knife hidden under her clothes, tried to stab me as I turned to leave. The old man went for my gun as I disarmed her,' Snipe grunted, pushing his way past them.

Danny stared at the man and the woman. The muscles in his cheeks flexed as he ground his teeth, his eyes narrowed and darkened with his mood. He turned and went after Snipe, grabbing him on the shoulder, spinning him around to plant a fist squarely into his face. The blow broke Snipe's nose and his wraparound shades at the same time.

'You murdering bastard,' Danny said.

Chaz and Smudge jumped in between them as Snipe moved in to retaliate, his nose crooked and bleeding.

'Fuck off, Pearson. I told you, they went for me. You'll fucking pay for that,' Snipe growled, gripping his nose to crunch it straight. He snorted the blood up and spat it on the floor by Danny's boots.

'Knock it off, guys, this isn't the time or place,' said Chaz, looking nervously around the compound.

Tension built as the two of them continued to stare angrily at each other for what seemed like an age.

'Let's go,' Danny finally said, leading the way back to the Land Cruiser.

The journey back to base took place in tense silence. Danny was brooding in the front passenger seat while Snipe sat in the back, his eyes boring angrily into the back of Danny's head. As soon as they were safely back at base, Danny headed straight to the camp commander, Major Blain McDonald, and reported Snipe's actions.

'Staff Sergeant Pearson, did you or any of your men

actually witness Sergeant Snipe's actions in the room, or have any proof that contradicts his account of the situation?'

'Er, well, no sir,' Danny answered. Now that he was calm, he could see he was on the wrong end of a no-win argument, with no chance of getting Snipe court-martialled for what he'd done.

'Then there is nothing more to say. We're living in turbulent times, Staff Sergeant. The war is getting a lot of bad press back home, and stories of soldiers killing innocent locals will do us nothing but harm.'

'So he just gets away with it?' Danny said angrily.

'Hold your tongue, Staff Sergeant, or I'll have you up on an insubordination charge. I was just about to say that Sergeant Snipe will be on a transport back to D-Squadron within the hour with my recommendation for a full psychological assessment. Between these four walls, it is an assessment he is unlikely to pass. Now, unless there is anything else, that will be all, Staff Sergeant.'

'Sir,' Danny said, turning and exiting the room, knowing that although he wouldn't get Snipe to answer for his crimes, he would at least get him drummed out of the military.

An hour later, Danny watched the chinook with Snipe on board rise above the camp in a cloud of dry dust before turning and heading off into the setting sun.

CHAPTER 10

Two Years After Project Jericho

Snipe walked out of the gate at RAF Hereford, home of the 22nd Special Air Service Regiment. Dressed in civvies, with his belongings packed into a large kit bag slung over his shoulder, he turned and walked along the busy A480 toward Hereford train station, five miles away. With no footpath, cars tooted as they passed him walking in the road.

'Yeah, stop the car and honk that horn shithead. I'll shove it somewhere where you won't hear it.'

He ground his teeth angrily as he walked and thought about being discharged from the SAS for being psychologically unstable.

'Pearson, fucking Pearson's done this for that shit in Afghanistan. I'll make that bastard pay for this.'

A car slowed behind him.

43

'Fucking overtake me, you arsehole,' Snipe shouted, waving the car past without looking back at it.

It didn't overtake, it just kept pace before giving a short toot on the horn.

'Right, that's it, you're fucking dead,' Snipe muttered, his face angry as he turned.

A large black Audi S6 sat behind him, the driver shrinking back into his seat at the muscular figure of Snipe moving angrily towards the car. The back door opened and a man in an immaculate pin-striped suit stepped out, his wavy blonde hair neatly cut into short back and sides. His ice-blue eyes focused on Snipe without a glimmer of fear in them.

'Good morning, Nicholas. Be a good fellow, put your bag in the boot and get in. We can have a little chat while we give you a lift to the train station.'

Snipe stared at him for a few seconds, deciding whether to get in or beat the crap out of him and the driver. Curiosity and having nothing to lose eventually made him chuck his bag in the boot and climb into the back of the car.

'So who the fuck are you then?' he said as the driver pulled away.

'Who I am is on a need to know basis, my dear fellow, and you don't need to know. For the purpose of this conversation, you may call me Howard.'

'Alright, I'll play along. What do you want, Howard?' Snipe said, his voice low and menacing.

'I'd like to offer you the opportunity to continue to serve your country.'

'Ha, right. In case you haven't heard, I'm a nut job, unstable, unfit to serve at Tesco, let alone serve my country. Now stop the car and let me out.'

'Now, now, Nicholas, we both know that's not strictly

true, and your, how shall we say it, unique problem-solving methods could be a distinct advantage in this particular area of employment.'

'Who do you work for, MI5, MI6?'

'No titles, and no limitations, dear boy. My job is to take care of the security of this country, by any means necessary, and that requires men who will get the job done, by any means necessary.'

Snipe stared at Howard as he thought the proposal over, his face eventually curling up into a big grin.

'Alright buddy, you're on.'

CHAPTER 11

Six Years Ago

Out of the military and still mourning after the tragic death of his wife and child in a hit-and-run accident, Danny was recruited by a special MI6 anti-terrorist unit hot on the heels of a cyber terrorist, Marcus Tenby. Rich and well connected, Tenby was using a crack team of mercenaries to eliminate his enemies while he put plans into place to crash the western world's financial systems.

Danny soon discovered that Snipe was one of the team of mercenaries. After missing them and Tenby in London, Danny and his team followed their trail to America and collaborated with the FBI in New York. Danny eventually tracked Snipe and Tenby to a disused garage in the Brooklyn Bay area.

Tenby escaped on a speedboat while Danny fought with Snipe. Hearing the police sirens in the distance, Snipe pushed him away and fled the scene, Danny gave chase.

Outside the garage, two cop cars were strewn sideways on the road, bullet holes riddling their windscreens. As one officer pulled his injured colleague to cover, Danny looked over at the petrol station. Snipe had punched out a tanker driver and climbed into the tanker's cab. Danny broke into a sprint and reached the back of the tanker just as Snipe ground it into gear. As it lurched forward, Danny grabbed for the rear ladder and got a handhold. The fuel pipe ripped off its coupling and a fountain of fuel sprayed across the forecourt from the back of the tanker. Danny hung, feet dragging along the road, then pulled himself onto the ladder and climbed to the roof. The tanker thundered along the road, following the bay.

A line of FBI and police cars dropped in behind it, snaking over the slippery fuel as it pumped out over the tarmac. Danny inched along the walkway on top of the tanker and dropped into the gap behind the cab. Taking hold of the grab bar on the back of the cab, he swung out wide, hurling a left fist through the open driver's-side window and connected hard with Snipe's cheek. The tanker swung to one side, bounced up the kerb, then slid back onto the road. Snipe turned to face Danny with insanity in his eyes as he grinned widely. He lurched the tanker hard to the left. Danny glanced forward in time to see an impending collision with a parked delivery van. He swung back behind the cab just as the tanker side-swiped the van. The vehicles bounced off each other in a scream of scraping metal.

Fragments of glass and plastic from the mirrors exploded from the impact. Danny looked back. The hose was still pumping fuel onto the road while a parade of cars gave chase. He edged across to the passenger-side grab-rail and felt around with his right hand for the door handle.

With a one-two-three count, he yanked the door open and swung himself into the cab. Snipe pulled his gun, forcing Danny to launch himself against the front windscreen and push Snipe's wrist away as he squeezed off a couple of rounds. The sound was deafening, and his ears rang as the shots blew out the passenger window.

Holding Snipe's gun arm back with one hand, he punched him in the kidneys with the other. It was like hitting a brick wall. Snipe pushed Danny's arm slowly back, twisting the gun towards his face. Danny headbutted the bridge of Snipe's nose. The cartilage collapsed on impact, and Snipe's face contorted as blood flowed from his nose and his eyes streamed. Danny grabbed the gun and twisted it out of his hand. As he turned the gun on Snipe, a boot planted in his chest, kicking him out through the passenger door. He threw his arms around wildly, hooking one through the windowless doorframe.

Turning his attention forward, Snipe saw the road bend sharply right with the glistening bay beyond it. He heaved on the steering wheel, fighting to make the corner. The tanker squealed and started to jack-knife before turning over. It flung Danny over a hedge and into the swimming pool of a bay-front holiday home.

Metal met tarmac, the sparks igniting the trailing fuel. A jet of flame accelerated towards the tanker and away down the road they'd come from. The chasing cars swerved out of its path, their wheels alight for a few moments until the fuel burnt off. Flames caught up with the tanker as it slid through the twin metal crash barriers between the road and the bay. The explosion peeled the tanker open like a sardine tin. A forty-foot-high fireball erupted from the destruction. The tanker hit the water a second later and sunk, leaving only a burning fuel slick in its wake.

Police and FBI cars screeched to a halt by the gap in the rails. The officers and agents cornering off the scene as they looked for signs of Snipe in the water. Behind the hedge, Danny pulled himself out of the pool and lay on the lawn, breathing heavily.

CHAPTER 12

Six Years Ago

With Snipe dead and Tenby's plans foiled, Danny and the unit returned to England, and Danny fell back into the normal routine of life. He headed for his favourite gym, Pullmans, owned by local legend Big Dave.

He pushed through the squeaky gym doors at 7.30 a.m.

'Danny,' Dave said casually, without looking up from the reception desk.

'Dave,' Danny replied, enjoying the ritual greeting.

'You back for long?' Dave said, slowly lifting his head to look Danny square in the eyes.

'So, it would seem.'

'You better fuck off and do some training then. You look soft as shit.' Dave dismissed him with a wave of his hand.

Danny chuckled. 'Yes sir.'

The gym was empty, apart from a young Lycra-clad woman standing on one of the running machines. She selected a playlist on her phone and nodded her head in time to the music, then fired up a treadmill. As she jogged, her blonde ponytail swished from side to side. Danny started to bench press weights, enjoying the feeling of muscle against metal as he added more weight to his work-out. The door to the gym squeaked open, and a large man in a baggy hoody entered reception. A baseball cap with its peak pulled low covered his eyes.

'Morning. You're not a member. Would you like to join, or would you like to pay as a guest?' Dave said, looking up from his computer screen.

The man tilted his head, displaying blistered skin covering the left side of his face. He grinned from ear to ear.

'Yeah, a guest. That'd be nice.' His head tilted again, revealing intense blue eyes. Dave remained motionless for a second, momentarily unnerved.

'How much?' the guy said.

'Five pounds, please. And you need to fill in a guest form,' Dave said, passing over a clipboard.

The man's arm whipped up, and a massive knuckle-dusted fist crashed into Dave's head like a steam train. Dave flew from his seat into the shelf behind. Tubs of protein powder and energy bars crashed around him. The man walked calmly behind the desk and reached up to the CCTV, switching it off. Dave tried to get up, but the man rained more blows into his jaw and nose. The guy stared at Dave's unconscious body, breathing heavily. He walked over to the door and locked it, flipping the closed sign around before tipping his cap back and heading into the gym.

Danny had worked his way up to 110 kilograms, then

sat on the edge of the bench while he caught his breath. He looked through the window that looked through to reception. The tubs, snacks, and drinks on the shelves were in disarray, and there was no sign of Dave. The hairs stood up on the back of his neck as alarm bells in his head rang. He sensed someone approaching within a hundredth of a second of catching movement in his peripheral vision. Approaching fast. Danny hooked his heels into the base of the bench and pushed back hard, sliding himself off the bottom. A cast-iron weight crashed onto the bench edge. It had missed Danny's head by millimetres, splitting the vinyl and foam cladding down to the metal frame. The crazed, scarred face of Snipe stood over the bench. Danny flipped into a forward roll, bumping painfully into the dumbbell rack. He looked back around to see Snipe grab a long steel bar from one of the lat machines, then come at him fast.

'Payback time, Pearson,' he growled.

Every man has a fight-or-flight instinct when his back's against the wall. Danny's was fight. He grabbed a dumb-bell from the rack and launched himself forward as Snipe took a two-handed swing. There was a terrific clang as the bar struck the dumbbell, the blow rendering them both motionless for a second. First to recover, Danny twisted to one side and gave two powerful kidney blows with his free hand. They should have dropped him like an elephant, but Snipe just folded to one side slightly before swinging the bar back fast. It caught Danny on his shoulder, knocking him over a bench and into a pile of stacked weights. The dumbbell flew out of his hand, clanging loudly against a cross-trainer. Ignoring the pain, Danny grabbed a steel weight, hurling it like a discus at the approaching Snipe, catching him squarely in the chest. The blow knocked Snipe backwards, the bar flying from his hand as he landed, sprawled between two rowing machines.

Ten feet behind them, the woman continued to jog on the running machine, her headphones on, unaware of the chaos behind her. Danny lunged forward, planting a sprinting-kick into Snipe's groin so hard that it slid him backwards. Snipe groaned and rolled back between the cycle machines before standing up, slightly bent over. His face was a mixture of pain, fury, and insanity. With a tremendous roar, Snipe lifted a cycle machine clean off the ground and threw it at Danny, catching him mid-torso and sending him flying back into the dumbbell rack again, the unforgiving hunks of metal digging into his back and ribs.

Fuelled with adrenaline, Danny grabbed a 10- kilo dumbbell and ran towards the rowing machines. He jumped high off its seat and drove the metal weight into Snipe's face. His nose exploded in a fountain of blood as he lurched backwards onto the empty treadmill next to the jogging woman. She looked across, shocked at Snipe's bloody form. Whipping upright, Snipe shook his head and looked back at her. He grinned and planted a fist into the side of her head, shattering her headphones as she bounced off the side bars of the treadmill like a pinball. Losing her footing, she hit the moving belt and catapulted out the back of the machine into a crumpled heap.

Desperate to keep the upper hand, Danny delivered another iron-clad punch to Snipe's head. But Snipe moved fast, dodging the blow to deliver an elbow to his ribs. He followed it with a blistering combination of punches to the kidneys and ribs. Danny crumpled, the wind ripped from his lungs. Snipe grabbed him around the middle, picking him up and charging forward, cracking Danny's head on a pull-down bar hanging from the cable of the tall multi-gym machine. Snipe slammed him down on the machine with a painful crack on the sliding-weight stack. Head spinning, Danny tried to keep his arms raised to block Snipe as he rained punches down on him.

'Ain't fucking golden boy now, are you?'

Every time Danny tried to get up, Snipe knocked him back down again.

'I've been waiting for fucking years for this,' growled Snipe. 'You should have seen your wife and kid's faces when I drove a fucking lorry over their car. Fucking classic.'

A numbness washed over Danny as the words hit him. He glanced left and spotted the locking pin in the multi-gym's weight stack. Fury replaced numbness as he yanked out the pin and punched it deep into Snipe's inner thigh.

'Argh, fuck!' Snipe yelled, dropping the weight as he grabbed his thigh. The machine's bar had dropped to the ground when Danny had pulled the locking pin out. Scooping the bar up, Danny cracked it over the side of Snipe's head, spinning the attached cable around Snipe's neck before twisting the bar behind his back. Shaking off the blow, Snipe clawed wildly at the cable as Danny leapt on top of the weight stack. It snapped the cable back into the machine, yanking Snipe up off his feet like a jack-in-the-box. Danny reached down and shoved the bloody pin back in at the bottom of the stack, engaging all the weights and his body weight to the cable around Snipe's neck. The cable tightened, cutting into Snipe's neck as he danced on tiptoes. His face burned red, veins bulging as he tried to suck air into his lungs.

Twisting around, Snipe grabbed the cable above his head and placed both feet on the side of the multi-gym. He pushed with all his might, lifting Danny and the stack of weights a foot off the ground. The scene stopped as though freeze-framed. Snipe's fury-filled eyes locked on Danny's. His face turned purple as his teeth ground together in hatred. Danny pushed hard against the top of the machine, forcing the stack back down and the cable to bite ever tighter into Snipe's neck. He watched as the tiny veins in the whites of Snipe's eyes ruptured. Finally, the man-mountain dropped, and his body went limp.

The weights stack clanged to their final resting place, and silence filled the room.

The police and ambulances were on the scene within minutes, with crews attending to Big Dave, the woman, and Danny. While police took statements, another ambulance crew untangled Snipe's body and wheeled it away into the back of the ambulance. They drove him away—no sirens or blue lights, no urgency. The patient was already dead. As they drove, the paramedic in the back of the ambulance did checks while he filled in the paperwork. He had Snipe's body hooked up to an EMS monitor displaying rows of flatline readings. The ambulance was only a few miles away from Whipps Cross Hospital when a rhythmic beep made him look up at the EMS monitor.

'Shit. Bill. Step on it, we've got a pulse.'

The lights and siren sounded as the ambulance picked up speed. Bill called in to A&E to warn them of their impending arrival. They were in sight of the hospital when a black Range Rover overtook them and cut in front, braking hard. A second black Range Rover moved up behind them as they slowed to a stop. Suited men climbed out of the back of the cars. They wore shades and talked over lapel mics, with earpieces hooked over their ears. They approached the driver's window, flashing MI6 identification up at the startled ambulance driver.

'Move into the rear please, sir, my colleague will be driving this ambulance to a secure location.'

'What? We've got to get this man to the hospital,' the driver protested.

55

'This is a matter of national security. Now get in the back and keep that man alive.'

The MI6 agent's suit jacket swung open to display a gun in a shoulder holster as he pointed the driver to the back of the ambulance.

'Ok, ok, I'm going.'

The agents got in, one in the driver's seat and one in the passenger's seat. The passenger twisted around and watched the paramedics intently as they worked to keep Snipe alive.

'Package is secure, sir, we're ready to move to the secure location,' the agent said into the mic.

'Affirmative, we're moving out,' came the response over the earpiece as the lead car pulled away. The other two vehicles followed closely behind.

CHAPTER 13

Four and a Half Years Ago

In the restricted wing of a military hospital, a patient's eyelids fluttered rapidly as beeps on the monitoring equipment beside him quickened. The eyes opened, and his pupils shrank as his bright blue eyes stared at the ceiling. He tried to pull the ventilator tubes out of his throat but barely had the strength to lift his arms that hadn't moved for eighteen months. A medical team rushed into the room and held him while they removed the tubes and checked his vitals.

'Keep calm, Nicholas. You're in the hospital. You've been in a coma for the last eighteen months. Just lie back and breathe normally for us, that's it. Do you know who you are?'

Snipe focused on the doctor, a frown appearing on his forehead as he tried to put his jumbled thoughts together.

'Yeah, I know who I am. What happened? Did that fucking sniper get me?'

'What sniper, Nicholas? What do you remember?' the doctor said, shining a little torch into Snipe's eyes.

'Er, the lead vehicle hit an IED and was blown to shreds. When we tried to help the gunner, a Taliban sniper started picking us off.'

'Where do you think you are, Nicholas?'

'Afghanistan, I told you, I'm alright,' said Snipe, trying to sit up before looking surprised that he didn't have the strength to. 'What the fuck is the matter with me? Am I paralysed, doc?'

'No, you're not paralysed. Just take it easy. You're in England, Nicholas, you had an accident and have been in a coma for the last eighteen months. Just rest, give it time. The team is here to look after you. I'll be along later to see how you're doing.'

The doctor left the room and headed down the corridor to his office at the end. He pulled Snipe's file out of the filing cabinet and laid it on his desk. The word 'Classified' was stamped in red across the top of it. He opened it and read the top page.

If the patient regains consciousness, call this number immediately.

Picking up the phone, he dialled the number. It only rang once before being answered.

'Case number, please,' came a woman's monotone voice.

The doctor's eyes flicked to the top of the file. '1-8-5-9-3-3.'

'Is the subject secure?'

'Er, yes,' the doctor said in surprise.

'Someone will be with you shortly.'

The phone went dead, leaving the doctor staring at the file, feeling like a spare part. Shaking it off, he replaced the receiver and put the file back in the cabinet before continuing his rounds.

In one of the many rooms within the Britannia Gentleman's Club in the heart of London, the government member known only as Howard sat at a private table, away from prying eyes and ears whilst he dined with a colleague. His phone rang. He looked at the number before putting it to his ear and listened. A minute later, he took it away and placed it back in his jacket pocket.

'I have a job for you, Simon.'

'Yes sir, what would you like me to do?' the government agent code-named Simon said enthusiastically. He was younger than Howard, an up-and-coming star in the agency and eager to climb the ladder to the top.

'You remember Project Jericho and the men I instructed you to keep an eye on?'

'Well, man, as I recall. Daniel Pearson is the only one left, but yes, I remember it.'

'That's not quite correct. The other man, Snipe, didn't die and has just come out of his coma.'

'Really? With or without all his faculties?' Simon said in surprise.

'He's reported to be functioning well but doesn't remember a thing about Daniel Pearson, Marcus Tenby, or New York. He still thinks he's on his first tour of duty in Afghanistan.'

'What do you want me to do?'

'Transfer him to Dr Fajarah's facility in Oxfordshire. Get them to rehabilitate him physically while the doctor works on his mind to keep those memories buried. Snipe's far too great an asset to just throw away,' said Howard.

'What if he goes rogue again?' Simon asked, his voice hushed.

'Then we'll terminate him. More tea?' Howard said, turning on a smile as he waved the waiter over.

CHAPTER 14

Present Day

Nicholas Snipe stepped off the plane and entered Istanbul Airport. He was barely recognisable from his former self, his once large, muscular frame now sinewy and athletic. The blonde military buzz cut was now neat, not too long and not too short, and a neatly trimmed beard sat below blue-rimmed glasses. Nothing remarkable, everything forgettable. He looked at the time and popped one of Dr Fajarah's pills into his mouth. They kept the headaches at bay, those and the large lump of missing memory being the only lasting effects of the coma.

It had taken eighteen months from when he awoke to get his body back into shape, followed by another year of specialist training before Simon would send him out on missions as a government asset. Two assassinations and a diplomat extraction later, Snipe was in Turkey to collect a suitcase from an Iranian scientist named Alboraz Hosseini. All he had to do was verify its contents via a secure video link on his phone, wait for the Iranian to confirm that his money had been transferred, then give him his new identity papers and leave. Snipe would then head to the port, where he was to catch a fishing boat called Ceylan and head out of Istanbul into the Black Sea. Later that night, they would rendezvous with a UK naval frigate that was patrolling the waters, hand the case over under the cover of darkness and head back to Istanbul where he would get a flight back to the UK.

He walked up to the counter at passport control and handed his cover passport over. Sven Magnusson, a Swedish-born architect from the UK didn't raise an eyebrow with the officer, who stamped it and handed it back with a bored look on his face.

He had no luggage other than a small bag slung over his shoulder and so he headed through the nothing-to-declare section into the arrival hall. As he rode down the escalators to ground level, a man travelling up on the escalator to his right caught his eye. There was familiarity about him, but he didn't know why. Sparks and neuro connections fired across his brain, causing a flashing headache across the right-hand side of his skull. Stepping off the escalator, Snipe stood to one side while the pain subsided. He turned and looked at the man walking away on the floor above. The feeling of familiarity was all he got, but the why still eluded him.

Shaking it off, Snipe headed out of the airport and took a taxi to the hotel where he was to meet the Iranian scientist. It was a large hotel, frequently used by tourists and business men and women from all over the world, all coming and going across the busy reception. No one took any notice of Snipe as he headed across the foyer towards the stairs to the hotel rooms. No one, that is, apart from a man with dark hair and Mediterranean features. He took a casual glance from behind his newspaper as he sat in one of the hotel chairs near the windows. Snipe spotted him the minute he entered the hotel, noting the giveaway English brogue shoes and Hackett London shirt in his peripheral vision.

Jesus, fucking amateur.

He wasn't surprised. He knew how Simon worked. Sending a backup asset in case something went wrong would be a natural precaution for him. Leaving the man behind, Snipe ignored the lift and headed up the stairs to the third floor. He pulled a hotel keycard out of his pocket. The meeting and the room access had all been taken care of by the agency. Rubbing his head as he approached room 232, Snipe fought against the stabbing pains bouncing around his skull. The man from the airport's face flashed up from somewhere in his missing memory. He looked much younger and was wearing a doctor's white smock.

Sliding the key in the lock, Snipe pushed the hotel door open and stumbled inside. He went into the bathroom and splashed cold water on his face. The image and pain passed.

'For fuck's sake, get a grip,' he muttered to himself before drying his face on a hand towel and heading towards the interconnecting door to room 234 in the bedroom's corner.

Pulling his side of the door open, he gave three taps on the adjoining room's closed door, then paused a couple of seconds before giving three more and standing back. There was a shuffling sound from beyond the room before the lock clicked and the door opened slowly inwards. A nervous-looking Iranian man peeped around the door's edge through little horn-rimmed glasses.

'Hosseini?' Snipe said bluntly.

The guy gave a nod and opened the door the rest of the way to let Snipe in.

'Have you got the case?'

'Yes, yes, it's here,' Hosseini said, pointing to the case on the bed.

'Ok, open it up. Once I get it verified, you get your money and papers and we go our separate ways,' Snipe said, his voice calm but authoritative.

Alboraz Hosseini moved ahead of Snipe and spun the combination barrels on the case before opening it up. Snipe didn't recognise the shiny cylinders, tubes and wires. But he did recognise the keylock to arm the device, a GPRS phone module with a SIM card holder and the small LCD screen, presumably to display a timer countdown.

Taking his phone from his pocket and pressing the dial button for a video call, Snipe waited for an operative at the agency to appear before turning the phone around to show him the contents of the open case for verification. Hosseini turned the key and the system lit up with a large beep, the LCD screen displaying various options in Arabic, followed by a set of signal bars as the cell phone unit received a signal. The beeping sound cut through Snipe's head like needles stabbing into his temples. Dropping the phone, he clutched his head. Drops of blood trickled from his nose to splash off a cylinder in the case.

'Hey, are you alright? Do you need a doctor?' Hosseini said, looking concerned.

The word 'doctor' triggered more lightning stabs in Snipe's head. Images of the man at the airport and memories of him from a research centre came flooding back. Like carriages pulling into the station, memory after memory arrived in a seemingly never-ending stream: Dr Heinrich Mann, the research project, Jones going off the roof, Fox setting himself on fire, Pearson getting him thrown out of the SAS, working for the government man, Howard, as an asset.

They just kept coming and coming: Howard trying to have him killed when he refused to do a job, driving a truck into Pearson's wife and child, killing for Marcus Tenby, New York, the tanker explosion, Pearson again, the gym fight followed by the endless darkness before waking up from the coma, the brainwashing and control and drugs to repress his memories at Dr Fajarah's facility, hours of mental torture overseen by Simon but under the orders of the government man named Howard.

Fury to the point of insanity hit Snipe. With a crazy look in his eyes, he focused on Hosseini. A small voice emanated from the phone by his feet, as the man from the agency shouted Snipe's name. The operative called for his superior as he watched and listened to Snipe muttering to himself as he advanced on Hosseini.

'Oi, egghead, what exactly is this thing?' Snipe growled menacingly.

'This is not the deal. You've verified it. Now I get my money and new identity,' Hosseini said, his voice cracking a little as he backed away from Snipe in fear.

'News update, me old china, there's been a change of plan. Now, I'm only going to ask you this one more time. What's in the case?'

'It's a hybrid nuclear device. The advanced technology makes it pound for pound the most powerful device ever made,' Hosseini said, hitting the wall when he ran out of the room to back away from Snipe.

'Device, as in explosive, a bomb?' Snipe said, grabbing the scientist's shirt in his fist and pinning him to the spot.

Hosseini nodded his head frantically.

'How powerful?'

'It has a ten-kilometre blast radius and would kill 90% of all life inside of seven kilometres.'

Snipe thought for a second, then turned his head slowly to look at the phone on the floor.

He'll be here soon.

Moving so quickly that Hosseini didn't see it coming, Snipe punched him in the ribs so hard he heard them break. With the wind knocked out of him and in agonising pain, Hosseini slid to the floor only to receive another blow to the temple, putting him out cold on the carpet.

'Take five, mate, I'll come back to you in a minute.'

The barely audible click of the hotel door on the other side of the interconnection made him cock his head. Snipe moved fast, running past the bathroom to pull the door to room 234 open as wide as it would go. He exited into the corridor, his footsteps silent on the carpet as he moved on his toes back to the door to 232. He tapped the key on the lock and slid inside. Moving in a circle, Snipe headed silently back to the interconnecting door, picturing the slow closure of room 234's door in his head as he moved up beside it. Rushing through, Snipe appeared behind the man from the foyer, his head and silenced Beretta moving from Hosseini on the floor to the noise of room 234's door clicking shut.

Snipe struck Simon's asset with a full body-weight punch to the back of his neck. His head whipped back as his body went down. Snipe kicked the Beretta away as the asset's hands hit the floor to save himself. As Snipe went in to finish him off, he moved like lightning, planting a kick to Snipe's stomach, sending him flying back into the kettle, teas and coffees. Springing upright, Snipe's face contorted as an insane fury took hold of him. He advanced on the asset as he spun up off the floor, pulling a commando knife from a sheath concealed behind his back.

'Come on then, pretty boy, let's see what you've got,' Snipe growled, his eyes wide and staring, a wide grin spreading across his face.

The asset lunged forward, aiming the razor-sharp blade at Snipe's torso. With his senses heightened and reactions accelerated, Snipe caught his wrist in a vice-like grip, pulling his arm to the side to power a crushing punch into the Adam's apple, breaking cartilage and the hyoid bone. The man stood dazed for a second before panic spread across his face as he realised he couldn't draw any air to his burning lungs.

'What's the matter, mate? You having trouble breathing? Here, let me help you,' Snipe said slowly, twisting the man's wrist inwards while curling his free hand over the top of the assets hand so he couldn't let go or drop the knife.

His eyes went wide in panic. He couldn't breathe or talk or stop as Snipe slowly forced the tip of the knife towards him. With one final, explosive movement, Snipe thrust the knife into his chest up to the hilt, twisting it ninety degrees to rip open the heart. He stood with a pleading look on his face for a few seconds, his whole body trembling before he collapsed limp on the floor.

Snipe pulled the knife out and wiped it on the corpse before turning to Hosseini.

'You, Hoosany, Houdini, or whatever your name is, can you change the language on that thing to English?'

'I, I, yes I can,' Hosseini said, terrified.

'Good, do it. Then I want you to tell me everything about that device.'

CHAPTER 15

hree men sat in a plain white-panelled van in a loading bay around the back of the hotel. They'd been driving around Istanbul all afternoon, returning to the hotel every hour until the police cars and media vans finally left the crime scene. An agent for the Iranian Secret Service, Darius Klek, appeared around the corner, looking both ways before returning to the van. He hopped into the passenger seat and closed the door.

'Did you find anything out?' the driver said, turning to look at him.

'Two dead, Hosseini and another man, no mention of the case,' Darius said.

'Any idea who he was?'

'No, the concierge heard the police say he didn't have any ID on him. Babak, has control got back to you yet?' Darius questioned, twisting around to talk to one of the men in the back.

'Not yet. They've hacked the hotel CCTV and are still going through today's footage.'

'Ok, let's move. Take us back to the hotel, Farid. We'll

rest up while we wait for information then decide what the next step is.'

Farid started the van and drove slowly through the city to a tatty, no-questions-asked hotel in the back streets of the city's outskirts. They had two rooms, but all sat in the one at the front of the hotel with a clear view of the approach road outside. An hour passed before Darius's phone finally rang.

'Yes.'

'The dead man is on our database as an asset for the British Secret Intelligence Service, Matt Sahin. He was killed by another man who flew in from the UK this morning under the name Sven Magnusson, a Swedish-born architect living in London. The passport and identity check out until you look further and find the man doesn't exist. I've sent you an enhanced still from the hotel CCTV, one of him leaving the hotel with the case.'

'What do you want us to do?' Darius said.

'Whoever he is, he's gone. He's probably left Turkey by now. Best guess is he'll head back to the UK to deliver the case. He can't get it through airport security, so he'll prob-ably go the long route, by sea and land. Use your Turkish IDs and visas and get yourselves on the next plane to London. Get ahead of him and await orders. We're running the image through several databases. I'll let you know as soon as we have identified him.'

The man hung up and Darius looked at his team looking back at him for answers, his phone pinging with the digitally enhanced photo of Snipe leaving the hotel with the case.

'Pack it up, we go to London to find this man,' he said, turning the phone around to show them a picture of Snipe.

CHAPTER 16

Thanks to the forward thinking of the agency, Snipe had emergency cash meant for a compromised mission, plus the cash and cards he got from Hosseini and the asset he'd killed. After splashing a few notes while talking to the locals in a Turkish market, one took Snipe to see his brother in a tucked away garage out in the suburbs of the city. Snipe paid over the odds for an old Mercedes taxi with 300,000 miles on the clock. A little extra money on the handshake ensured there was no paperwork with the sale. Wasting no time, Snipe drove sixteen hours straight, only stopping for fuel and caffeine drinks on his journey across five borders, eventually ending up in Graz, Austria. He'd used his Sven Magnusson passport, not caring that it would get flagged by the agency.

He was ahead of the game. It would take them time to track him and longer to get men in place to intercept him, plus they didn't know where he was going. With the return of his memory came the knowledge that he had money, plenty of money, and identities—passports, driving licences and bank accounts—hidden in safety deposit boxes, self-storage centres and bolt holes across the world. His time as a government asset and as a mercenary wiping out targets for Marcus Tenby had paid very well.

At 10 a.m. he parked a hundred metres short of an unremarkable four-storey block of apartments overlooking the River Mur. Stifling a yawn, Snipe reached into his backpack, pulled out the asset from Istanbul's silenced Beretta and tucked it under his jacket as he got out. Memories of meeting the agent to rent the ground-floor apartment as a safe place to run to if he ever needed it came flooding back. The rent would have long since defaulted while he lay in a coma, but needs must. He entered the foyer, checking that the stairs leading up to the other flats were clear before walking to the corner flat. Snipe knocked on the door, his other hand holding the Beretta out of sight under his jacket.

A man in his twenties answered the door, looking up at Snipe as he smiled back, saying nothing.

'Can I help you?' the man said in German.

'Put the kettle on, chum, I'm parched,' Snipe chuckled back, whipping out the Beretta from his jacket followed by a metallic ping as he put a bullet in the man's forehead.

Stepping over the body, Snipe shut the door and headed for the kitchen, poking his head into the lounge on the way to check it was clear. He put the Beretta on the kitchen worktop and flicked the kettle on, riffling through the cupboard until he found the coffee and sugar. He'd just fetched the milk from the fridge when a voice came from the bedroom.

'Who was at the door, Otto?' she said in German.

Snipe put the milk down and picked up the Beretta. 'Your worst nightmare,' he muttered, a sadistic grin spreading across his face.

Half an hour later he left her on the bed, her neck

snapped at an odd angle, her mouth gagged with her own underwear, and a pair of tights tied around her head to keep them in place, while another pair tied her wrists behind her back.

Snipe made himself the coffee he'd started earlier, took a swig, and sighed. Putting the cup down on the kitchen worktop, Snipe tapped the stud wall between the kitchen and the living room, stopping when he heard the hollow sound of the space between the upright studwork. A smile formed on Snipe's face. He took a step back and planted a powerful kick into the plasterboard, smashing a large hole into the cavity. Kneeling down, Snipe shoved his hand up inside the void and pulled a sealed, black plastic bag out. Dumping it on the kitchen table, he took another swig of coffee and then opened it, thumbing through the different passports, credit cards, ID, cash and safety deposit keys, the memories of their acquisition becoming more vivid with every item he looked at.

Draining the last of his coffee, Snipe put everything, including the Beretta, back into the black bag. He turned all the gas hobs and oven on without igniting them before walking casually away from the hissing gas and headed towards the front door. He ducked into the lounge on the way out and turned the gas fire on. Driving off with a trail of diesel smoke behind the old taxi, Snipe looked in the mirror just in time to see the explosion blow the windows of the tiny apartment out, the fireball curling up past the first-floor apartment, the blast wave setting off a cacophony of car alarms.

Desperately needing sleep, Snipe headed into the city, stopping at a chemist on the way. He parked at random, leaving the car unlocked with the keys in the ignition. He walked, carrying the case and his backpack, to the first hotel he came across, checking himself in using one of his old identities. After examining the room and sliding a chair under the door handle, Snipe entered the bathroom and opened the bag from the chemist. He took out the razor and shaving foam, removing his beard but leaving the moustache. When he'd finished, he mixed up the at-home hair dye, changing his hair and moustache colour from sandy blonde to dark brown. After he had dried his hair, he combed it over with a parting down the left. Finally, he put on a pair of the mildest strength reading glasses he could find in the chemist and looked in the bathroom mirror, holding up a passport under the name Henry Patterson with the five-year-old picture of him in the same disguise. He was older and thinner in the face, but he matched the picture of his younger self well, plain and ordinary looking, forgettable.

Tomorrow he would buy another car and some suitcases, and clothes to go in them. Then he'd put the metal case inside one suitcase, pack clothes around it and in the other suitcase, before driving to Calais, France, where he would get on the Eurotunnel back to the UK. Exhausted, with voices, images and pain spinning around in his head, Snipe stripped and fell into bed. He was asleep within minutes.

CHAPTER 17

The four-strong Iranian Secret Service team got off the Gatwick Express train at Victoria and made their way to an Airbnb apartment booked by the agency. It was private and discreet, with a coded lock entry, so they didn't have to meet anyone to let them in. They'd just settled in when Darius's phone rang.

'Yes.'

'The man who has our suitcase is Nicholas Snipe, ex-special forces and Secret Service asset for the British government. He disappeared off the grid four years ago. I've sent his files to your phone,' Darius's handler from the agency said.

'So the case is in the hands of the British?' Darius said, expecting to be ordered home, as they were too late.

'We don't think so. We've intercepted a cell transmission from within MI6 to an operative known as The Hawk. They think Snipe has gone rogue, and have authorised The Hawk to retrieve the case before terminating him. MI6 has tracked Snipe from Istanbul to Austria, where they found the car he was using abandoned in Graz. This supports the theory that he's trying to make his way back to England.'

'What do you want us to do?' Darius said.

'I've sent you an address. Ask for Ali, he works for us, he will supply you with weapons. In Snipe's folder there is a list of addresses he's been known to use in the past. Check them out. If you see him, kill him and get the case, but be careful. The British Secret Service and The Hawk will also be looking for him.'

'Ok,' Darius said, hanging up.

Opening the first secure file, Darius transferred it to his laptop and opened it while the team crowded around. The file on Snipe was five years out of date and full of blacked-out, redacted paragraphs, giving them only a vague description of Snipe's army career, followed by a section titled Project Jericho. The following five pages were blacked out apart from words like to, the, and them.

'Have you ever heard of Project Jericho?' asked Babak.

'No, but this name Daniel Pearson keeps popping up in Snipe's service record, and here again in Project Jericho, and again here, where Snipe's decommissioned from the SAS.'

'We should get the agency to track him down,' Kaveh said, looking over Darius's shoulder.

'I agree, get on it, Kaveh,' Darius said, opening another file full of Snipe's known past addresses. 'Farid, find us some transport. We'll go and see this Ali and get some weapons. Then we wait. Snipe was in Austria last night, he can't fly with the case, so he'll have to come here by land, sea or Eurotunnel. Either way, the earliest he can be here is tomorrow morning. We'll start checking the addresses out then. If we get information on this Pearson, we'll check him out as well.'

'He's lost a lot of weight,' Babak said, looking at the

service picture of Snipe and the enhanced still from the hotel in Istanbul.

'Yes, but you can still tell it's him. He's gone out of his way to look forgettable. We have to assume he may change his appearance and identity again. Study this photo, facial shape, bone structure and body type. I want every one of you to be able to recognise him from a glance.'

'Yes sir,' they said simultaneously.

CHAPTER 18

t took him a lot longer than expected to find a cheap car to buy, and by the time he'd bought suitcases and the clothes to fill them and cover the smaller metal case, it was well into the afternoon. Snipe removed the radio and wedged his silenced Beretta deep inside the dash before replacing the radio. Satisfied, he set off for Calais, France. Memories and dark thoughts tumbled through his mind while voices jabbered inside his head as he drove.

'They fucked you, mate,' came a voice, clear as day.

'Who has?' Snipe muttered as he drove.

'All of them. Fucked with your head, pumping all that shit in your veins. You know what I'm talking about.'

'What, the research centre?' Snipe said out loud.

'Damn right the research centre. Look what happened to Walters, Jones and Fox. They fucked them too.'

'You're right, that's where it all went wrong. They messed with my head. That fucking General Cracknell, and the doctors, Heinrich Mann, Mandrell and Kapur.'

'You should do something about it, make them pay.

You're Nicholas Snipe. Nobody fucks with you or your brother.'

'My brother? Terrence. Yeah, no one fucks with the Snipes. I'll see Marco. He'll know where Terry is.'

The voices drifted away, leaving Snipe thinking, plotting, and brooding about what he'd do once he got back to the UK. After driving through Austria, Germany, and Belgium, he entered France. He hit a large service station a few miles outside of Calais at around two in the morning. Pulling up in the far corner of the car park, Snipe turned the engine off, put the seat back, and caught a few hours of sleep.

In the morning, he went inside the services, used the toilets to freshen up, and made sure his appearance still matched his passport. He bought four pay-as-you-go phones from an electronics shop in the terminal before getting two breakfast rolls and a coffee from Subway. Feeling refreshed, Snipe used one of the phones to buy a ticket for the next Eurotunnel crossing.

Two hours later, he drove through the automatic entry gate and pulled up at passport control. It was a busy day, and he was in the middle of a constant flow of cars moving steadily forward to get on the train. If MI6 had alerted the authorities, they would have been all over the vehicles, checking all the occupants. Instead, the customs officer just waved him through without a second glance. Just over an hour later, it was the same story at the Folkestone terminal. They waved him through and he exited the terminal onto the M20, heading towards London. Around two in the afternoon, Snipe pulled up outside Marco's father's business, Binelli's Motor Services. He got out, stretched, yawned and headed towards the garage workshop.

Marco Binelli had worked for his dad since he left school and was Snipe's brother's best mate. Even when

Terry went to prison, Marco kept in touch with him. Snipe asked a young trainee where Marco was and got directed toward the noise of a whining air ratchet coming from the far side of a Mazda.

'Hello Marco,' Snipe said, looking at a short, stocky man tightening the wheel nuts. Marco looked older and more like his dad than the last time he'd seen him.

'Hello, er, how can I help? Wow, fuck me, Nick?' Marco said, a look of surprise on his face when he finally recognised him.

'Yeah, it's me,' Snipe said with a grin.

'Bloody hell, you look so different. Where have you been? We all thought you were dead,' Marco said, moving over to Snipe and shaking his hand.

'Long story. I'm looking for Terry. Is he out of prison? Have you seen him?'

'Terry? Shit, Nick, you don't know?'

'Know what?' Snipe said, his face darkening.

'Sorry Nick, I hate to be the one who tells you, but Terry's dead,' Marco said, his eyes falling to the floor.

Snipe looked at Marco, his blue eyes staring intensely as he processed what Marco had said.

'What happened?'

'When Terry heard you'd been killed by some fucking war hero, Parish? Parson?'

'Pearson,' Snipe growled.

'That was it, Pearson. Anyway, Terry went mental. He broke out of prison and chased this bloke, Pearson, all over London trying to kill him. It all ended in the underground car park of that Sky Garden building on Fenchurch Street. Armed police shot Terry when he wouldn't give up. I'm really sorry, mate.'

Snipe's face went taut as he ground his teeth and

clenched his fist, fighting to keep his growing anger in check.

'Where is he?' Snipe said, after a few deep breaths.

'He's up at the East London. They buried him next to your mum.'

'Thanks Marco, you were a good friend to Terry. Look, if anyone comes asking about me, I was never here, ok?' Snipe said, giving Marco a nod before turning and walking away.

'Sure, mate. Good to see—' Marco said, his voice trailing off at the end when he walked around the car to find Snipe nowhere in sight.

―――――

Snipe walked around the outside of the East London Cemetery, his eyes cutting across to the section where his mother and brother were buried. No one looked out of place, and there were no suspicious vehicles nearby, so he made his way over to their graves. He looked at his mother's for a while, then at his brother's. Reaching into his pocket, he pulled out a bullet and stood it on top of the gravestone.

'I'll make them pay, Tel. I promise I'll make them pay for you and for me,' he said out loud.

'That'll work better if you put it in a gun,' came a voice from the left, a voice he knew well.

'You're dead, Tel, a figment of my imagination,' Snipe said, looking across at his brother, grinning back at him.

'That I am, little brother. But dead or not, you need me. We've got work to do, debts to pay. There's a long list of people who've screwed us both over, starting with those fuckers who treated you like a lab rat and ending with the one who gave you a near death and who killed me. Pearson. We'll save him until last.'

'Where do we start?'

'You saw him in Turkey, that wanker in charge of research at the centre.'

'The doctor. Heinrich Mann. First we need to see the man who ran that research project. He'll know where they are.'

'Yeah, you're right, we need to find General Neil Cracknell.'

'Find him and I can find out where they all are and what he did to us all,' Snipe said, picking the bullet back up off the gravestone and walking away. He turned after a few feet and looked at Terry's image.

'You coming?'

'Too fucking right, bruv, I wouldn't miss it for the world. The Snipe brothers back together again,' Terry said with a wide grin.

CHAPTER 19

'Get the door, love,' Danny shouted from the sofa, his arm in a sling from a healing bullet wound to the shoulder, and feet up on a pouffe to ease the pull on another healing bullet wound to his stomach.

'Ok, ok, coming. What did your last slave die of?' shouted Nikki, smiling at him as she headed out of the kitchen to open the door.

'I killed them for answering back,' Danny chuckled.

'What was that?' Nikki shouted back.

'Nothing, dear,' Danny replied.

He heard her laugh from the hallway, then voices as she greeted Danny's brother Rob, his wife Tina, and their four-year-old daughter Sophie, who came running into the lounge to jump on the sofa and hug Danny.

'Woah there, kiddo,' Danny said, feeling a little pain when she put her weight on his stomach.

'Are you alright?' she said, blinking her bright blue eyes at him.

'I am now. How's my favourite niece?' Danny said, hugging her back the best he could.

'I'm ok,' she said, giggling. 'How did you hurt yourself?'

'Uncle Danny fell over on holiday, Sophie,' said Rob, walking in.

'You should be more careful,' she said, looking back at Danny.

'Yes I should,' Danny said, watching her run off to see what Nikki and Tina were up to in the kitchen.

'Alright, bruv, how are you really feeling?'

'Pretty good, Rob. The stomach only hurts when kids jump on it, and the shoulder's healing nicely. The sling's only for Nikki's sake. I'm under strict orders to take it easy. What can a man do?' Danny said, smiling at his brother.

'She's good for you, Danny. How are the wedding plans coming along?'

'Cheers Rob. We're hoping to get married late summer. Nikki's flying back to Oz the week after next to get her house on the market. Hopefully it'll sell quick. Then she'll be back here and we can book the wedding date.'

'I still can't believe you're getting married to little Nikki Miller, Scott's sister. I remember winding her and her friends up when we were at school,' said Rob, picking Sophie up as she ran back into the lounge.

'Yeah, and I still owe you for that,' said Nikki, following Sophie into the room ahead of Tina.

'Hello Tina, how's it going? All alright with the baby?' Danny said, looking at her pregnant belly.

'Everything's fine. We're just waiting for a niece or nephew to join the family,' she said, smiling at Nikki, who blushed and looked at Danny.

He smiled back, trying not to think about his first wife and son, killed some years ago by Nicholas Snipe. 'Well, you never know,' he finally said.

The sound of Scott's Porsche pulling up outside broke the awkward silence. They all looked out the window at

Scott getting out of the car in an Armani suit, a bottle of bubbly in one hand. His floppy, sandy-coloured hair bounced as he walked around the car and opened the passenger door to help a stunningly beautiful blonde woman out.

'How does he do it?' Danny said, shaking his head.

'She's got to be ten years younger than him. Oh shit, here he comes,' Rob said, as Nikki went to the door and everyone else turned away from the window and made out they weren't staring.

'Hello sis, how's the invalid?' Scott said, giving his sister a hug.

'He's on the mend, in the lounge.'

'Forgive me, this is Yasmin. Yasmin, this is my sister Nikki,' Scott said, before wandering into the lounge. 'Robert, Tina, you're looking well. Daniel, you look moderately ok, I suppose.'

'Thanks mate, love you too,' Danny chuckled.

'Everyone, this lovely young thing is Yasmin. Yasmin, this is Robert and his wife Tina, my god-daughter Sophie, and that's Daniel. Be wary of him. He spends most of his time either trying to kill me or save me. I'm never quite sure which,' Scott said, chuckling.

'Oh, Daniel, you're the man Scott saved from the evil cartel in Colombia single-handedly. I hope you're feeling better now,' Yasmin said, looking at Danny.

'Er, yes, well, anyone for a drink,' Scott said, flapping at his over-exaggeration of the Colombian adventure.

'Yes Yasmin, I'm feeling much better, thank you. Scott's a real hero. He saved my life. I don't know what I would have done without him,' Danny said, letting Scott off the hook, much to his amusement.

The day flowed with drink, food and good company, putting Danny in a great mood. Scott brought some more beers in as Danny sat with his brother in the lounge.

'So, where did you meet the lovely Yasmin then, Scott?' Danny asked.

'Ah, at a rather select dinner party. She's a ballerina from the Royal Ballet troupe, very talented and very flexible,' Scott said with a smile.

'I'm sure she is, Scotty boy. God knows what she sees in you.'

'I'll have you know I'm considered a bit of a catch,' Scott replied, frowning.

'If you say so, mate.'

'Anyway, enough of that. When are you going back to work, old man? You can't sit around here forever,' Scott said, changing the subject.

'Mmm, not sure I am, Scott. I'm going to see Paul next week, and I'm thinking of quitting. I've got some money saved and I just want to take some time out, marry Nikki and enjoy some time with nothing happening—no fights, no guns and no injuries. I came too close to buying it in Colombia. Next time, I might not be so lucky,' Danny said, his injuries grumbling as he moved, emphasising the point.

'Perhaps you're right, old man. Let's face it, you're not getting any younger,' Scott said, turning as Yasmin walked over, sat on the arm of the sofa, and slid her arm around Scott's shoulders.

'Look who's talking. You're older than me, mate,' Danny said, looking at Rob and chuckling.

'Yes, but the years have been considerably kinder to me than you,' Scott said with a smile and a wink at Danny.

'You know what? I can't argue with that,' Danny replied, raising his beer can in a nod to Scott.

CHAPTER 20

eneral Cracknell drove in through the electric gates and headed up his shingle drive to the house. It was dark, and the outside lights were on. He parked up under the floodlight above the garage, which flicked on as he approached and got out. Walking briskly to the front door, he went in and shut the door behind him. The house was unusually dark inside, the only source of light coming from around his office door which was open a crack.

'Sandra,' he called out.

With no answer, he moved to the office and pushed the door open. A man sitting behind his leather inlaid antique desk smiled back at him, a silenced Beretta in his hand, aiming at the general's head. As the door opened further, Sandra came into view. She was standing on tiptoe on a chair, her ankles gaffer taped together and wrists taped behind her back. She looked at him, her eyes wide in terror as she let out a muffled scream through her taped-up mouth. Her stockinged toes were desperately trying to keep balance on the chair, while the rope tied to the heavy chandelier pulled tight, looping in a noose around her neck and keeping her from putting her feet flat on the chair's soft cushion. The general moved to save her.

'Stay where you are, General,' Snipe said, pointing the Beretta at his wife.

'Let her go. What do you want?' The general said, stopping in his tracks to look at Snipe.

'Eight army volunteers, the research centre, Dr Heinrich Mann. I want to know the truth, everything. Who commissioned it, what you did to us, everything.'

Cracknell took a good look at Snipe, finally seeing through the age, weight loss and disguise. 'I know you. Nicholas Snipe. You'll never get away with this. Let my wife go,' he ordered.

Snipe picked up a paperweight off the desk with his free hand and threw it at Sandra, hitting her in the stomach, making her jerk and dance around as she struggled to keep her balance, the rope cutting deeper into her neck.

'Ok, ok stop. It's in the safe. I'll get it, just don't hurt her,' the general said, moving with his hands up passively.

He moved to one of the wooden squares on the panelled office wall and pressed it. It popped open on a hinge to reveal a safe behind it. Spinning the combination lock, the general opened the heavy door and flicked through the bundle of files inside, sliding one out and handing it to Snipe. As Snipe looked down at "Project Jericho, TOP SECRET" written on the front, the general darted his hand to the back of the safe to grab a Glock 17 tucked out of sight. As he brought his hand back out, Snipe grabbed his wrist with one hand and throat with the other, hoisting him off the floor before dumping him down into his office chair.

'Oh, General, it's all too much for you, mate. Your missus has topped herself and you can't live without her,'

Snipe said, forcing the general's hand with the gun across until it pointed under his chin.

'Fuck y—' the General started to say, his words cut short as Snipe, sliding his finger over the general's trigger finger, pulled down. The bullet entered under the chin before blowing the back of the general's head out all over the wall behind them. As he slumped back into the office chair, Snipe opened the file and flicked through the contents.

'Is it all there?' his brother said from the chair in the room's corner.

'Yeah, everything,' Snipe said, the general's wife looking down at him, with tears streaming down her face, terrified by this lunatic who'd killed her husband and was talking to himself.

Snipe shut the file and headed towards the door.

'Oi, bruv, aren't you forgetting something?' Terry said from behind him.

'What? Oh yeah,' Snipe turned, looked up at the general's wife and gave her a big grin.

'Don't worry, love, I'm letting you go,' Snipe said, giving a wink at his dead brother's image before putting the gun away and clicking a flick knife open.

He slid the sharp blade through the gaffer tape around her ankles, peeled it off her stockings, and put it in his pocket before doing the same with the tape on her wrists. Lastly, as she danced on tiptoe to keep balance, he peeled the tape off her mouth and pocketed it. Staring up at her, Snipe slid his hands up her legs, grinning as she tried helplessly to wriggle out of the way.

'For fuck's sake, bruv, get on with it, I'm getting bored,' Terry said inside Snipe's head.

'Alright, you fucking killjoy,' Snipe grumbled, looking up at Sandra.

In a flash of anger, Snipe kicked the chair out from under her. She dropped a few inches, stopping abruptly as the rope around her neck snapped tight, crushing her windpipe. She kicked and jerked, her eyes bulging and face going purple as Snipe watched, his eyes twinkling with morbid satisfaction.

'Take it easy, Sandra,' he said, when she stopped moving.

Instantly bored with the situation, Snipe picked up the file and walked casually out of the house.

CHAPTER 21

Darius Klek and his team pulled up outside Binelli's Motor Services in a van stolen from Gail's Bakery chain earlier that morning. He looked across at the workshop and down at the list the agency had supplied him, with all known contacts for Snipe, past and present.

'Let's go. Kaveh, Farid, hang back by the entrance to the workshop. Babak, you come with me,' Darius said as they all exited the van.

They walked over to the workshop where Farid and Kaveh stood on either side of the loading door. Darius walked in with Babak trailing a few feet behind him, his eyes darting around all corners of the workshop.

'Excuse me, is Marco Binelli around?' Darius said, his English only slightly accented.

'Who's asking?' said a short, stocky man, eyeing Darius suspiciously, a heavy torque wrench in his hand.

'Detective Hammed, Interpol. I'd like to know if you've seen a man named Nicholas Snipe recently,' Darius said, flashing his fake Interpol ID.

'Nick, Christ, I haven't seen him for years. I can't help you, mate. Now if you don't mind, I've got a busy morning,' Marco said, dismissing Darius and turning back to the car he was working on.

Darius caught the nervousness in Marco's eyes and the overly quick way he responded, like he was prepared for someone coming to ask.

'No, I don't think that's strictly true. Is it, Mr Binelli?'

Marco turned and stood up slowly, the wrench still in his hand. 'You calling me a liar, pal?' he said aggressively, his father and two other lads from the garage hearing it and moving closer from around the cars.

'Oi, dickhead, if my son says he hasn't seen him, he hasn't seen him. Now I think you better leave while you've still got the legs to carry you,' Marco's father said, picking up a tyre iron off the bench as he stood in front of Marco to snarl at Darius.

'Ok,' Darius said, taking a step back before sliding his hand in his jacket to draw a Glock handgun. He shot Marco's father in the thigh, sending him to the floor, screaming in agony.

The two other lads turned to run out of the workshop, only to find Kaveh and Farid had moved inside of the door and were now pointing guns at them.

'Now, Marco. I want you to tell me everything you know about Nicholas Snipe, what he looked like, where he was going, everything, because if you don't, I'm going to put a bullet in your father's head, just before I put one in yours.'

A few minutes later, Darius and the others walked back out of the garage. They turned and walked across the road to the van.

'First, we check out this flat Snipe used to own in Shadwell, then we ditch this van and get a new one,' Darius said, as he and Babak crossed the road and walked around the back of the van, preparing to get in and leave.

Two policemen stood in front of them with the van driver's door open, their focus moving away from the punched-out door and ignition locks to look at Darius and Babak.

'You two stay exactly where you are. Now place your hands on the side of the vehicle. You're under arrest for the theft of this motor vehicle.'

'Of course. Babak, do as the officers say,' Darius said in a calm voice, smiling as he raised his hands and turned to face the side of the van.

Instead of placing them on the side of the van, he grabbed the handle of the sliding side door and pulled it open.

'Sir, stop what you're doing,' the officer said, moving towards Darius.

Before he got near him, Farid and Kaveh had circled around the other side of the van out of sight and appeared behind the officers. Kaveh grabbed one around the neck while pushing the barrel of his gun into his back. Farid reached around and held a razor-sharp hunting knife across the other officer's throat.

'Handcuffs please, gentlemen,' Darius said in a calm voice while pulling his gun to cover them.

'You won't get away with this. Do yourselves a favour and give up now,' the officer said as Kaveh and Farid cuffed their hands behind their backs and pushed them on top of the bread trays in the back of the van.

'Change of plan, Farid. You drive the van back into the garage.'

Farid did as Darius asked, parking it in the middle of the cars and ramps and the bodies of Marco, his father, and the two mechanics.

'Babak, find the keys to that BMW,' Darius said, pointing at a blue BMW X4.

'Look, let us go, mate, don't make things worse for yourselves,' the officer said, his voice cut off when Kaveh slammed the side door of the bakery van shut.

While Babak drove the BMW out of the workshop, Farid and Kaveh walked out and got in the back and Darius undid the welding torch from the oxygen and acety-lene tanks with a spanner. He spun the valves open, walking away from the high-pressured hiss to a bin by the roller door on the far side of the workshop. Picking up an oily rag from the workbench, Darius pulled a lighter from his pocket and lit the rag, dropping it into the bin full of paper, cardboard, rags, and rubbish. He stepped out of the workshop, hitting the close button as he went, the bin's contents catching well with flames whipping out its top by the time the roller door hit the floor.

'Let's go, he said to Babak as he climbed into the passenger seat.

Babak wasted no time and drove out of the garage, heading for Snipe's old flat in Shadwell.

Inside the bakery van, one of the policemen managed to roll away from his colleague and was feeling for the transmission button on the radio.

'That's it, Dave. Up a bit more. You got it, now press.'

The radio cramped into life.

'Officer 284 to control. Officers in distress. We need help, over.'

'Go ahead, officer 284. What is your situation? Over,' the trained calm voice of a control room operative came back.

'They took us at gunpoint while investigating a vehicle robbery. We're handcuffed in the back of a stolen bakery van inside Binelli's Motor Services on Church Road, Shadwell.'

'Sit tight, officers are on their way. ETA four minutes. Are the gunmen still on site?'

'I don't think so. We heard the roller door close and a car drive away,' the officer said, straining his ears to hear any sound outside of the van.

'Can you give us a description of the gunmen?'

Before the officer could answer, the acetylene gas reached the burning bin, and a massive flash explosion ripped through the workshop, incinerating the van with police officers in before blowing the walls out and collapsing the roof down on top of them. By the time the police cars turned up, all that was left was a smouldering pile of rubble.

CHAPTER 22

Dr Heinrich Mann left the podium to rapturous applause, his talk of the advances in neurological science and drug treatments for degenerative diseases like dementia and Alzheimer's going down well among the other doctors at the convention held at the Hilton Hotel, Stuttgart. When the day's talks ended, Dr Mann shook hands and chatted with other eminent doctors in the foyer, before heading up to his room to shower and change into more appropriate clothes for the night's black-tie gala dinner.

Tapping the card on the door of his sixth-floor hotel room, he entered, puzzled to see the maid had drawn the curtains when she made the room up, leaving it in darkness. He popped the card in the power slot and turned on the lights, jumping back as they illuminated Snipe sitting in a turned-around chair by the dressing table to face the doctor as he entered the room. Snipe sat cross-legged in white paper overalls, complete with the hood up over his head, thick yellow rubber gloves, and yellow wellington boots. The silenced Beretta was held loosely in his lap, pointing up at the doctor's head. On the bed beside him, Snipe had laid a towel from the bathroom down and placed a variety of knives, tape and bone saws he'd stolen from a nearby veterinary surgery.

'Hello Doc, remember me?' Snipe said in a low, gravelly voice, his piercing blue eyes staring intensely as his mouth curled up into a wide grin.

'No, I don't. What is this, some kind of sick joke? Get out of my room,' Heinrich answered as confidently as he could, still holding on to the hope this was some crazy junior doctor prank that would see him as the butt of the joke for years to come.

'No? Doc, now you're hurting my feelings. Why don't you come over here and sit down while I remind you?' Snipe said, rising from the chair with the gun Heinrich had thought to be a toy raised in front of him. A gun that now looked very real, inches from his forehead. 'Sit.'

'What do you want?' Heinrich said, his voice cracking as fear gripped him.

'Project Jericho,' Snipe said, pushing him into the seat.

The doctor's eyes flicked from the gun to Snipe. The man in front of him was thinner and older, his beard and the hair poking out from under his hood were a different colour, but the eyes were the same, piercing blue with an intensity that made it hard to hold his gaze.

'Nicholas Snipe,' he whispered back.

'Bingo, we have a winner,' Snipe said loudly, holding out his arms before swiping the butt of the Beretta into the doctor's temple with tremendous force, knocking him on the floor out cold.

'Come on, bruv, get on with it. I'm getting bored.'

'Well, if you'd like to get off your arse and help me, Tel, it'd get done a whole lot quicker,' Snipe said, looking across at the vision of his brother sitting on the bed frowning at him.

'You're even crazier than I thought. How can I help you? I'm fucking dead, you idiot,' his brother growled back.

Snipe looked at his brother's image while reaching for the gaffer tape, then burst out laughing. He was still laughing as he picked up the doctor and dumped him in the chair, taping his hands, feet, and torso to the chair's frame. When he'd finished, he put tape across the doctor's mouth and sat on the bed, waiting for the doctor to come round.

He eventually got bored and, picking up a coffee cup by the room kettle, headed to the bathroom and filled it up. When he returned, he threw the water in Heinrich's face and stood back. He watched with delight as the doctor came round, shock, surprise and fear rolling across his face as his mind caught up with his predicament.

'Wakey, wakey, Doc, now this is what's going to happen. You and your quack friends pumped our heads full of shit, you fucked my head up, and all the others bar one killed themselves. That makes you worse than me in my book, and you've got to pay the price, me old china,' Snipe said, turning away from Heinrich to pick up a shiny bone saw off the bed. Turning back, he let it glint in the spot lights overhead and grinned.

'Now, Heinrich, my old friend, I won't lie to you. This is going to be an agonising death. But suck it up, mate, you've got no one to blame but yourself.'

As Heinrich did a muffled scream into the tape gag, Snipe stepped behind him and gripped his hair tightly in one hand to stop him from thrashing his head around. With the other hand, he placed the bone saw on the side of Dr Mann's neck and pushed the surgical steel teeth deep into his neck. There were a few seconds of Heinrich jerking and straining his taped body against the chair before the saw severed the carotid artery, spraying Snipe's overalls, boots, gloves and the room in a fountain of blood. Snipe laughed and continued sawing as Heinrich's blood pressure bottomed out and the spray turned into a slow ooze. He eventually sawed clean through the vertebrae and held Heinrich's head up to face him.

'There, that wasn't so bad, was it? Here, Tel catch,' Snipe shouted, throwing the doctor's head to his dead brother, only to watch it go straight through his image to bounce on the bed before rolling onto the floor. 'Butterfingers.'

'Fuck off, wanker,' Terry growled.

'Alright touchy,' Snipe chuckled back, before writing the word 'Jericho' on the wall in large letters using Heinrich's blood.

'You're going to let them know you're coming?' Terry said.

'I want them to know. They can't stop me. I'm like the avenging angel, Tel. You can't escape me.'

'Avenging angel, nice. I like that, bruv. Now let's get the fuck out of here.'

CHAPTER 23

anny headed up the old wooden staircase to the third floor and to his place of work, Greenwood Security. He usually ran up the stairs three at a time, but with the healing bullet wounds to his stomach and shoulder still grumbling, he took it at a fast pace. Pushing through the creaky oak door, Danny entered the office.

'Morning Evie,' he said to the new receptionist, giving her a smile as he headed towards his office.

'Morning, Mr Pearson, good to see you looking better.'

'Thank you, Evie, and for the hundredth time, just call me Danny,' he called back over his shoulder, then worked his way through the office as the staff all greeted him, pleased to see him recovering.

Paul Greenwood, Danny's boss and close friend, came to his office door as Danny approached.

'Jesus Paul, are you paying this lot to be nice to me or what?' Danny said, accepting Paul's warm handshake when he reached him.

'What can I say, you're a popular guy. Come into my

office,' said Paul, turning back to his desk. 'You just missed Edward.'

Edward Jenkins was the Director of the Secret Intelligence Service and, although never officially linked, both Paul, his security company, and Danny had worked for him many times.

'Yeah, what did he want?'

'Oh, he was just passing and popped in for a social chat. He's been looking into a garage explosion in Shadwell. Coffee?' Paul said, getting his secretary's attention and mouthing coffee while pointing between himself and Danny.

'Yes, please. Yeah, I saw that on the news, oxy-acetylene cylinders went bang or something. But why would Secret Service be looking into that?' Danny said, puzzled.

'There's something the reporters don't know. The four garage workers found in the debris were killed before the explosion took place, and someone parked a stolen van with two handcuffed policemen in the middle of the garage before they blew it up.'

'Bloody hell, any leads?'

'Four men seen speeding away in a car just before it went up. It's a bit vague, but serious enough for Edward to get MI6 all over it.'

'I'll bet. Thanks,' Danny said, as the new trainee, Adam, brought the coffees in.

'Anyway, that's enough about that. How are you feeling? Are you coming back to work? You look a lot better,' Paul said, changing the subject as he took a swig of coffee and frowned. 'Oh god that's bad. I don't know if that trainee's going to work out.'

'Er, yeah,' Danny pulled a face and put the cup down. 'Look, about coming back, I don't know how to say this, but I don't think I will be.'

'Oh, er, ok. How come?' Paul said. His concern for his friend way outweighed any need for him to return to his job.

'Colombia, that's how come. I've used up all my lives, mate. I came too close to not coming home at all, and nearly lost Nikki and Scott at the same time. I just want to marry Nikki and opt out of things for a while, no pressures, no dramas, and no nearly getting killed.'

Paul sat looking at Danny for a while before speaking.

'Then I think that's exactly what you should do. But don't quit your job. Call it an extended leave of absence. Your job is always open if you ever want to come back.'

'Thanks, Paul, you've always been a true friend,' Danny said, getting up to shake his hand.

'I'll be expecting an invitation to the wedding then,' said Paul with a smile.

'Of course, it goes without saying,' Danny smiled, heading out the door.

'Don't be a stranger.'

'I won't,' Danny said, turning back to give him a grin.

CHAPTER 24

'Hurry up, Baz, the doors will shut in a minute.'

The last in a group of twenty-something men leaped through the Tube train doors as they slid shut. They laughed loudly, thumping down into the seats along the side of the underground Tube train as it moved out of the station.

'Oi, dickhead, that's my brother's seat,' came a low gravelly growl from the seat opposite.

The six men looked across in unison at the man across the carriage sitting with his head tilted down, his features hidden by a hoodie pulled up over a baseball cap, his elbows resting on his knees and hands clasped loosely together.

'Fuck you talking about, ain't no one here,' Baz said, the alcohol filling him with false bravado.

'And who you calling dickhead, eh? You wanna watch yourself, talking like that. You're liable to get your head busted,' his mate chipped in. The six of them, all young, dumb, and full of Friday afternoon booze and too much testosterone, stared angrily across at the man as he sat perfectly still.

'I'm talking to you, shit stain. You're in my brother's seat. Now fucking move,' Snipe said, his head tilting up just enough so they could see his gritted teeth, newly clean-shaven face, and his piercing blue eyes as he looked up from under the peak of his cap.

'Shut the fuck up, you crazy old bastard! Ain't no one else here,' Baz said, looking to the others and shaking his head while pointing at Snipe.

Snipe cocked his head to look at his brother standing by the door, looking down at Baz.

'What are you waiting for, Nicky boy? Fuck this little shit up,' Terry said with a smile.

'Right you are, bruv,' Snipe replied, his head coming fully upright as his focus moved back on Baz, a wide grin spread across his face.

'Who's he talking to? Fucking freak belongs in a loony bin,' one of Baz's mates said, making the others laugh and shout insults in Snipe's direction.

There was an explosion of superhuman movement as Snipe went from sitting to the other side of the carriage in a split second. He grabbed Baz's pointing finger, snapping it backwards out of its joint to point towards his wrist. Before Baz could register the pain, Snipe followed it with a fist to the bridge of his nose, shattering the cartilage and sending Baz's head smacking back loudly on the carriage window behind him. Instead of pulling the fist back, Snipe lent in and folded his arm, driving his elbow sideways into the temple of Baz's mate sitting in the next seat, knocking him unconscious.

There was a tug from behind him as one of the lads grabbed the back of Snipe's hoodie in his fist, pulling the hood and cap off Snipe's head to reveal a blond crew cut underneath. Dropping to his knees, Snipe threw his hands up and shot forward, leaving the hoodie hanging loose in the man's hands. In a snap movement, Snipe jumped to his feet and spun around. The mixture of insanity and fury on Snipe's face made the younger man drop the hoodie and back away further down the carriage. His mate stood his ground and drew a knife, holding it out in front of him with growing confidence.

'Come on then, let's fucking have it,' he shouted, as much to psych himself up as to intimidate Snipe.

Snipe just chuckled, stamping his foot down on the metal floor to make it boom as he jumped forward, the sudden movement forcing the guy to swipe the knife in an attempt to keep Snipe back. The move was clumsy and predictable. Snipe caught his wrist and pushed it out to the side, grabbing the upper arm with his other hand. He pushed the guy's arm around one of the poled uprights in the carriage, throwing his body weight forward to bend the elbow joint the wrong way until it popped and snapped around the pole, leaving the man screaming, his arm flapping about uselessly.

Snipe stood and stared at the three remaining mates, backing their way up as far in the carriage as they could get. He was just about to go for them when the Tube train slowed for the next station. Stooping down, Snipe grabbed his hoody and hat off the floor and threw them back on, walking out the opening door with his head down to avoid the station cameras.

Up on street level, he moved through the stream of pedestrians, checking reflections in cars and shop windows to see if anyone was following. Satisfied that he was alone, he headed toward his old flat in Shadwell. Crossing the road casually instead of turning down it, Snipe glanced the hundred metres down the road to his front door. Something bugged him about it. He kept walking straight on as he processed the mental snapshot of the road. The parked BMW near the flat. He was sure he'd seen two heads above the front seat headrests.

A little further on he entered the park that ran the length of his road all the way to the parade of shops on the far end, just past his flat. Snipe walked across the middle of the park, turning and running for the edge where the trees and bushes that grew just inside the iron railing boundary obscured any view from the road beyond. He pushed his way into the hedge, just far enough to see the road on the other side. The BMW sat twenty metres away with two men in the front, dark-haired with Middle Eastern looks. Snipe's eyes scanned past the flat towards the parade of shops. Another Middle Eastern man sat on a bench, pretending to read a newspaper. A fourth one appeared at the top of the stairwell to the flats above Snipe's flat.

'The flat's burned,' Terry whispered beside him.

'It doesn't matter. The case and my stuff are safely tucked away in the self storage unit. We'll go carry on with the plan and go to Mumbai,' Snipe said, pulling himself back out of the hedge to walk casually back the way he came.

CHAPTER 25

The government man, known only as Simon, walked briskly through Hyde Park, his breath billowing like smoke in the cold February morning air. He followed the path that ran alongside the lake and headed to a bench near the top. Simon sat down next to a middle-aged man in a suit, his face buried behind a copy of the Financial Times. He brushed a bit of fluff off his heavy winter coat with his leather-gloved hand and gazed across the lake at the Princess Diana Memorial Garden.

'Good morning, Simon. What news do we have on the Istanbul incident? Have your man and the case been recovered yet?' said the voice from behind his paper.

'No, General, I'm afraid they have not. In fact, the situation may have gotten rather worse.'

'How the hell could the situation get any worse? We have an Iranian scientist killed on Turkish soil while trying to sell us the world's most powerful compact nuclear bomb,' the general said, folding his paper neatly.

'It would seem Nicholas Snipe may have had somewhat

of a relapse,' Simon said, discreetly handing a brown envelope to the general.

'What's this?' he said, opening it and sliding out some photos of a decapitated corpse sitting in a chair, the word Jericho written in large letters in blood on the wall behind him. 'Jesus, who the hell is he?'

'Dr Heinrich Mann, he was the head geneticist for the Jericho project.'

'When and where?' the general said.

'Stuttgart, Germany. The coroners put the time of death somewhere between 6.00 and 8.00 p.m. last night.'

'Jesus, poor sod never stood a chance.'

'Unfortunately there's more,'

'Go on.'

'I got a call on my way here. General Neil Cracknell has been found at his home with his brains blown out and his wife hanging from the chandelier beside him. It's staged to look like he shot himself after his wife committed suicide. But after Stuttgart, I think we can both agree this is more than likely Snipe's handiwork.'

'Yes, it would seem so. He's going after everyone involved in Project Jericho. What about the others?'

'I've got men watching three of them and Pearson. It's been ten years since we disbanded the project. The others are pretty spread out. Don't worry, we'll get him.'

'I'm not the one who should be worried, Simon. I voiced my reservation about using that lunatic Snipe months ago. The committee, and your predecessor, the Minister of Defence, are baying for your blood. I suggest you resolve this and resolve it quickly. Maybe you should put Pearson on it?'

'Unfortunately, Pearson is convalescing after being injured in Colombia. I have another contractor already in the field. One of the best, code name The Hawk.'

'Ah, the Serbian, excellent choice. Get it sorted, Simon. Put Snipe in the ground, and get that briefcase back, and do it quickly.'

'Yes General,' Simon said.

An awkward silence followed until the two men got up and left the bench, walking in opposite directions, seemingly unconnected to all around them.

CHAPTER 26

The freelance asset for hire, known internationally as The Hawk, moved through the streets of Mumbai. A short but thick black beard covered old scars from the war in Bosnia many years ago. He'd been caught in an airstrike and only survived because an English special forces soldier had pulled him out of the rubble and carried him two miles to the nearest hospital. The soldier had been Danny Pearson. Their paths crossed again some years later, when a corrupt general had paid him to kill Danny. The Hawk had disregarded the order and repaid the debt to Danny.

Spotting his target as he left the medical college where he worked, The Hawk followed at a safe distance, sweating profusely in the thirty-degree oppressive heat. They walked along the two-mile route towards his target's apartment. It was located in one of the many tall, modern and clean buildings spreading along the left-hand side of a main road. In stark contrast, the famous slums of Mumbai spread away into the distance on the opposite side of the road. He watched the man enter the apartment building, his legs disappearing out of sight through the glass entrance door as he climbed the stairs.

Looking around, The Hawk took a seat outside a bar with a clear line of sight to the entrance door. He ordered a drink. Once the waiter had left, he took his phone out and studied the pictures of Snipe and the other Project Jericho members on his list. Lieutenant Henry Thomas and Sergeant Gary Burns were in a safe house in the UK and being watched by Simon's men, which left Dr Vihaan Kapur in the apartment opposite and Dr Samantha Mandrell in Cape Town.

The Hawk had been in Goa when the contract landed, so it made sense to go to the closest first. Personally, he doubted Snipe would show. He'd have to be crazy to try to kill the remaining people on the list with so many people after him.

Inside the building, Dr Kapur slid the key into the apartment lock and went inside.

'Hi Kashvi, I'm home,' he said, hanging his coat on the hook before taking his shoes off.

'Kashvi, Aahan,' he called again when his wife didn't answer.

He froze when he reached the doorway to the kitchen. His wife Kashvi and teenage son Aahan faced him, heavily taped to kitchen chairs behind the table. They tried desperately to shout through their gagged and taped-over mouths, but only muffled groans came out. A hockey puck-sized disc was taped to the centre of both their chests with wires leading to the hand of a figure standing behind them.

'Hello Doc,' Snipe said, a grin spreading across his face, his bright blue eyes burning excitedly.

The doctor's eyes fell on a handgun placed in the middle of the kitchen table. He dived forward and grabbed it, moving it around in his shaky hands as he tried to get a lock on Snipe as he ducked down chuckling, keeping himself tucked in behind the doctor's wife.

'Careful Doc, one press of this button and those little explosive devices are going to turn your loved ones' insides into their outsides,' Snipe growled, holding up his hand with the detonator in.

'Ok, ok, don't hurt them. Who are you, what do you want?' the doctor said, placing the gun shakily back down on the table.

'Doc, I'm hurt. Don't you recognise me?' Snipe said, moving back out from behind Kashvi.

'No, I don't. Please, take anything you want. I have a little money, you can have it. Anything, just don't hurt my family,' Dr Kapur said, tears running down his panicked cheeks.

'Project Jericho ring any bells?'

The doctor went very still, his eyes staring at Snipe until they went wide when recognition kicked in.

'There we go, now you remember,' Snipe said slowly.

'What do you want?' Dr Kapur said, his voice less shaky than before.

'Unlike when you pumped my blood full of shit, I'm going to give you a choice, Doc. You can pick that gun up and shoot me, but not before I blow your wife and kid's hearts out of their bodies. Or you can put that gun under your chin and pull the trigger, and I let them live. Scout's honour,' Snipe said, grinning as he held the detonator up and danced his thumb on the top of the button.

'You're crazy, but, but, you can't be serious.'

'Tick tock, Doc, I'm not known for my patience. What's it going to be, save yourself or save your loved ones? But hurry because I've got either a plane or a funeral to catch, depending on how this goes.'

The doctor looked between Snipe's grinning face and

that of his terrified wife and child as they shook. Tears streamed down their faces. With a shaky hand, he picked up the gun and slowly moved it up under his chin.

'I'm sorry, I love you,' he blubbered, tears and snot running down his face.

His wife shook her head and screamed into the gag just as the doctor pulled the trigger, blowing the back of his head out over the kitchen wall behind him.

'Woo hoo, good on ya, Doc, I didn't think you'd have the balls to do it,' Snipe said, giving Kashvi a slap on the back before moving forward to pick the gun up off the floor.

'Right, I'll be off then.'

'Aren't you forgetting something?' his brother Terry said, leaning against the back wall.

A grin spread across Snipe's face. 'Hang on, yes Tel, there was something else I needed to do. What was it?' Snipe said, with an exaggerated thinking look. He rubbed his chin with the hand holding the detonator before looking at it and grinning. 'Oh yeah.'

He pulled the kitchen door forward to stand behind it in the doorway and pressed the detonator button. There were two loud pops as the small explosive charges went off, instantly liquidising everything in Kashvi and Aahan's chest cavities. They stared back at Snipe as he took a peep back through the smokey haze left by the detonated devices, faces locked in shock until their brains caught up with their dead bodies and their heads flopped forward.

CHAPTER 27

The Hawk heard the gunshot but didn't react. To the untrained ear, it sounded like a backfire or construction noise. He also heard the loud pop of the explosive devices going off a few seconds later. He was less sure what they were but knew they were related and that the doctor was almost certainly dead. He took another sip of his drink, watching the entrance door while not staring directly at it. Snipe emerged, shades and baseball cap pulled low to hide his features. As The Hawk took another sip, he made sure he sat relaxed like a tourist and didn't look straight at him. Snipe turned his head in a full sweep of his surroundings. His eyes locked on The Hawk immediately, and he was on the move before The Hawk had time to put his drink down.

Shit.

Exploding out of his seat, The Hawk set off in pursuit, his eyes locked on Snipe as he ran across the main road, weaving through Mumbai's famously choked-up traffic of cars, tuk-tuks, black and yellow taxis and beaten-up delivery vans of all sizes. Conscious of his orders, under no circumstances was he to kill Nicholas Snipe until he retrieved the stolen metal case, The Hawk left his gun tucked out of sight in its holster under his armpit and ran after Snipe, straight into the cacophony of horns and swerving vehicles. He made it across the road just as Snipe disappeared into the dark, narrow alleyways of the slums.

The Hawk ran after him, dodging around the locals, living, working, and cooking inside and spilling outside of their tiny block and corrugated metal sheet, square hovels. He followed the flow of parting people up ahead, their heads turning as Snipe charged ever deeper into the squalid, stinking shacks. Using the advantage of the opening gap made by Snipe, the Hawk sped up, closing the distance until he could see Snipe's baseball cap as he ran head and shoulders above the locals. The peak darted to the side, and Snipe vanished down an alley to the left. The Hawk slid on the dirt and littered floor, knocking a local man flying as he changed direction and headed after Snipe, leaving the angry shouts behind him.

Snipe ducked out of sight down another alley ten metres up ahead. The Hawk followed to find the alley opened out into a small square with four alleys leading off it. Three-storey block and corrugated buildings surrounded the square, and Snipe was nowhere to be seen. An old man sat between stacked-up clay pots, busily spinning the next one on his potter's wheel. He eyed The Hawk nervously, his eyes flicking to the building opposite before looking back down to his pot. The Hawk turned to look at the building, with highly stacked bags of sorted recyclable plastic bottles and flattened, tied bundles of cardboard on either side of its open door. He drew his gun and moved cautiously inside. If it came between orders and getting killed, he'd kill Snipe in a second.

More stacks filled the darkness of the ground floor. A

single bare bulb hung from the centre of the wooden-boarded ceiling, offering only a smattering of light between the stacks. He slid between them, moving silently with his gun up in front, whipping around the back of each stack to empty space before moving forward and repeating the process, working his way towards the rear of the building.

A low chuckle floated in the air, causing him to stop. He focused on keeping calm and listening for movement, ignoring his heart thumping hard in his chest. A noise behind him made him whip around, only to find the gap between the stacks empty.

Edging to the corner of another stack, The Hawk spun around to find Snipe standing right in front of him. Both men moved like lightning, grabbing each other's wrist of their gun hand as if it were choreographed, pushing the guns out to the side as they both pulled the triggers. Bullets ripped into the stacks on either side of them as they spun around, locking on to each other until both guns clicked empty. Both men instantly released and launched into a Krav Maga style of fighting with elbows, punches, knees, and kicks. Their arms and legs were a blur of attacks and blocks as they bounced off the rocking stacks, The Hawk getting in blows here and there to no effect. Snipe came back harder and faster every time, his teeth gritted and eyes focused insanely on The Hawk's. His strength waning, The Hawk jumped back and spun around a stack, moving back and weaving into the dark at the back of the room. He reached down and pulled his trouser leg up, sliding a serrated hunting knife from a sheath strapped to his shin.

'Come out, come out, wherever you are,' came Snipe's growl, followed by another chuckle.

Regaining his composure, The Hawk edged his way through the stacks, stopping every few feet to listen for the telltale signs of movement. He heard the sound of rustling plastic as Snipe brushed a stack nearby. Before The Hawk could dart around to attack, Snipe shoulder-charged the stack in front of him, toppling it onto him. He fell back, causing the stack behind him to topple over as the domino effect worked its way down the line, trapping The Hawk on his back between them. Before he knew what had happened, Snipe had both hands on his arm, snapping his wrist back as he ripped the knife from his hand. A split second later, Snipe pushed the tip on the soft part of The Hawk's throat below the Adam's apple just hard enough to pierce the skin.

'Alright matey? Now, who do you work for then?' Snipe said in a jovial tone.

The Hawk just stared back defiantly. He knew how this ended and there was no way he was going to give Snipe anything.

'What's the matter, cat got your tongue?'

'Fuck y—' the Hawk started to say, the razor-sharp knife sliding easily into his throat until the tip hit his spine, taking his voice.

Snipe gave it a quick jerk left and right to sever the windpipe and carotid artery. A sea of blood flooded down The Hawk's windpipe, drowning him in his own blood before he bled out. All he could do was watch Snipe wipe the knife on him and stand back grinning, before leaving him to choke and shake, then lose consciousness and die.

CHAPTER 28

'Mmm, you're feeling a lot better,' Nikki said, lying in bed next to Danny just after they'd made love.

She ran her soft hands over his many scars to the fresh one on the side of his belly button.

'Yeah, my stomach doesn't hurt much anymore. The shoulder's still pretty stiff though.'

'That's not the only thing that was pretty stiff this morning,' she said, smiling at him.

'Steady, girl. It's only been six weeks. You're likely to put me back in hospital,' Danny chuckled.

Nikki leaned over and kissed him before hopping out of bed and walking into the en-suite for a shower.

'What time is your flight?' Danny called after her.

'Half three,' she called back over the noise of the shower.

'You sure about this, selling the house and moving back to the UK?'

'Yeah, I've had my time in Oz. Besides, I've got dual

citizenship. If you moved to Australia, you'd have to go through the whole immigration process.'

'I suppose so,' Danny said, getting out of bed.

'That is, unless you're having second thoughts,' she said, taking her head out of the stream of hot water.

The shower door opened and Danny walked in, sliding his hands around her as he kissed her neck.

'The hot water's good for my shoulder. It's feeling stiff again.'

'Oh, so it is,' Nikki said, looking down, then up with a smile.

Later that day, Danny drove Nikki to Heathrow and waved her off on her flight. He drove back home at a leisurely pace, enjoying his BMW M4 and the music on the stereo. A black Mercedes caught his attention three cars back. It moved when he moved, overtook when he overtook, always three cars back, classic tailing training.

Frowning, Danny took a sharp left, gunning the powerful car as soon as he was around the corner, then braking heavily to take the next left. He powered down the road again, breaking and turning at every new opportunity, giving his tail no hope of keeping the line of sight and following him. Disturbed but satisfied he'd lost them, he doubled back to rejoin the road home.

When he reached his road, Danny drove past, circling the block twice. Satisfied that no one was there, he parked outside. Entering the house, he stood in the hall, listening to the sounds of the house. Nothing. All quiet apart from the usual tick of the central heating and hum of the fridge freezer. Like a light switch being thrown, Danny ran up the stairs to the bedroom. Opening the wardrobe, he threw the shoes out and hooked his finger in a small hole at the rear. Pulling the false bottom up and out, he checked that the sports bag full of money still sat in the metal-lined box sunk into the floor. Pushing it to one side, Danny pulled out a loaded Glock 17 handgun. He quickly slid the panel back, and chucked the shoes on top, shut the wardrobe, and went back downstairs. He sat on the sofa and looked out through the blinds at the road out front.

Holding the gun loosely in his hand, he rested it on the sofa beside him and sat there motionless, breathing calmly, his eyes locked on the road outside. An hour later, the black Mercedes pulled up outside. Two men in black suits sat unmoving in the front. Danny stayed motionless, waiting for them to make the first move.

Fifteen minutes went by, and still no one moved. Danny heard a sound from the kitchen, an alien sound, a metallic click. The door. He was up quickly, moving to the hall, gun up, sharp, focused eyes looking along the sights. He moved towards the kitchen, hearing the kettle start to boil noisily as he approached.

'One sugar lump or two, Mr Pearson?' came Simon's familiar voice.

'I told you I'd put a bullet in your head if you ever broke into my house again,' Danny said, lowering the gun and walking into the kitchen to see Simon dropping tea bags into two of his mugs, one of his men standing just outside the back door.

'That you did, Daniel, but needs must, dear boy,' Simon said, looking at him with the teaspoon of sugar above his cup.

'One. What's this all about, Simon?'

'We have a problem.'

'There's no we, Simon. You have a problem. I don't want to know,' Danny said, scowling at Simon as he sat down at the kitchen table.

'Nicholas Snipe,' Simon said, placing the mugs of tea on the table.

'He's dead. I killed him, so what?' Danny answered bluntly.

'I'm afraid that's not exactly true,' Simon said, pulling a thick file from the inside pocket of his jacket and placing it on the table.

'What the hell do you mean that's not exactly true?' Danny said, flipping the file open to see a picture of an older, slimmer version of the man he killed years before. 'How is this possible? I killed the bastard.'

'I'm afraid the man just won't stay dead,' Simon said, sitting back to sip his tea while Danny spread the photos across the table.

'I know this guy from years ago, an MoD research project. Snipe was there, General something, er, Cracknell. General Neil Cracknell. Who's the headless guy, and what's Jericho?' Danny said, looking up at Simon.

'Dr Heinrich Mann, and Jericho was the official name for that rather unfortunate ill-fated research project.'

'Snipe killed them?'

'Yes, it would seem he's on a personal quest to take revenge on all the people he blames for his miserable life. One would imagine that you would be high up on said list,' Simon said matter-of-fact like he was discussing the weather.

'What? But why now? Where's he been all these years?'

'After your little altercation with Mr Snipe in the gym, the ambulance crew got a pulse. They moved Snipe to a secure military hospital where he remained in a coma for over eighteen months. When he came around, he had no memory of anything after his first tour of Afghanistan. With the help of a very talented doctor and medication to keep his less desirable traits under control, we kept it that way, built him back up, trained him, and put him out to work as a government asset. Unfortunately, on his last assignment, it would appear Mr Snipe regained his memory, bringing us to our present situation.'

'Christ, when will people ever learn? Why invest so much into one man? Why didn't you just let him die?' Danny said, picking up the report on the Jericho project.

'None of my doing, my dear fellow, this all stems from my predecessor, Howard, the now Secretary of Defence Mr David Tremain's time. Project Jericho was the dream child of Dr Heinrich Mann. He got the general on board, and the general sold it to the government, who put Howard in charge of overseeing it. It was all rather embarrassing for all involved, what with illegal genetic engineering and millions of taxpayer's money spent, only to result in six dead soldiers and a nutcase. A complete failure, well, apart from yourself, that is. They kept Snipe alive because of your success. If they could control his mind, they would have another you.'

'You bastards pumped me full of shit and lied to me. Why the fuck should I care what Snipe does? You're lucky I don't kill you and give him a hand,' Danny said, his face hardening as he glared at Simon.

'Ah, but you won't, will you, Daniel? You're not a psychopath like our friend Snipe. You always do what's right. And don't forget, you killed him, he'll be coming for you and your loved ones,' Simon said, holding Danny's gaze.

They sat in the kitchen in silence, the tension weighing heavily in the air until Danny finally spoke.

'So what do you propose?'

'You know Mr Snipe better than anyone. We know you're recuperating, so we'll give you all the men and resources you need. Help us find him and eliminate him.'

Danny sat and thought some more before finally nodding his head. 'Ok.'

'Good man. There's just one other thing.'

Danny locked eyes with Simon once more, not hiding his dislike for the man. 'Go on.'

'When Mr Snipe had, shall we say, his relapse, he was on an assignment. He took a rather important metal case. It's imperative we get it back. Be a good chap and retrieve it for us.'

'What's in it?'

'Nothing to concern yourself with, items of national security, that sort of thing.'

Silence filled the air again, the tension only broken this time by Simon getting up to leave.

'Right, I'll send a car for you in the morning at 8.00 a.m. Mr Jenkins has an incident room booked for us at the Secret Intelligence Service building. I'll see myself out.'

Outside, Simon's car pulled up in front of the black Mercedes with the two agents in. Just as Simon stepped out of Danny's house, the driver hopped out and moved around to open the passenger door for him. Once inside, Simon dialled the number for his predecessor, once known only as Howard, now known as David Tremain, the Secretary of Defence.

'Simon.'

'Mr Pearson is on board, sir.'

'Good, and he knows about the case?' David said.

'Yes sir, only that it is imperative that it's retrieved. Should I call off The Hawk?'

'No, the more people we have on this the better.'

'Very good, sir,' Simon said as the driver pulled away.

'Keep me informed of any updates on the situation, any time, day or night.'

'Very good, sir,' Simon said, hanging up.

CHAPTER 29

After finding nothing at Snipe's flat, they moved on to the only other connection they had, Danny Pearson. They turned onto his road and parked well away from the house, sitting there for five minutes, looking for anything out of place. Satisfied there wasn't, they were about to get out when Danny drove past them. He continued straight past his house and turned out of sight at the end of the road.

'Do we follow?' Farid said.

'Wait,' Darius ordered.

Moments later, Danny had completed his loop around the block and turned back onto the road. It was obvious he was looking for something in particular, as he gave them only a passing glance, disregarding them before parking outside his house.

'Are we going in after him?' Babak said from behind the driving wheel.

'No, we wait. Farid hand me the sight off the sniper rifle,' Darius said, flicking his hand up over his shoulder as Farid tapped the powerful sight into his palm.

123

An hour ticked by slowly until a black Mercedes approached from the far end of the road and stopped near Danny's house.

'Two men, they look like Secret Service agents,' Darius said, seeing the men's faces in the crosshairs of the sight like they were sitting right next to him.

A few minutes passed before another car turned onto the road. It stopped short of the house, keeping out from view of the front window. The suited front passenger and driver got out and the driver scooted around to the rear passenger door and opened it. Darius watched the man who got out closely. He straightened his expensive tailored suit before reaching back in to fetch a thick file from the back seat. He said something to the driver before turning and disappearing down the alley leading to the rear of the house with the man from the front passenger seat. The driver got in and reversed the car away before doing a three-point turn and driving away.

'I know him. He's the head of the UK's Security Council. Code name Simon.'

A little time later, Simon came out the front door, and the cars drove off. Seconds later, Danny walked out the front door holding a file, the butt of a Glock 17 clearly visible tucked into the waistband of his jeans. He paced to the edge of the kerb and looked down the road in the direction the cars had driven off. As Darius focused on the back of his head, Danny turned to face his way, his eyes looking straight down the sniper sight at Darius, making him flinch it away.

'There's no way he can make us out from this distance,' Darius said out loud as if to convince himself.

He put the sight back up to his eye and looked again. Danny stared in his direction for a few seconds longer before turning and walking back inside his house.

'I want to know what's in that folder.'

'Let's go and get it then. Farid and I can take the back. You and Babak take the front,' Kaveh said from the back.

'No, Kaveh, I know what sort of man this is. He is not someone you can rush in on. He's on guard, ready for action, and in a place he knows. To rush him now would result in several if not all our deaths. We will come back in the early hours while he sleeps. No, let us go now. I have to report this to control.'

CHAPTER 30

Danny wasn't sure if he heard, sensed, or felt a presence in the house. His eyes were wide open, and his hand on the Glock under the pillow next to him inside of two seconds. He squinted, the alarm clock hurting his eyes with its red LED display reading 3.05 a.m. Lying motionless, he listened to the sounds of the house. Nothing stood out as odd. But still, he had the nagging feeling something wasn't right. He moved across the bed, ready to slide off closest to the door. Without turning a light on, Danny put a leg out and carefully touched the carpet with his toes. Letting his foot slowly fall until it was flat on the floor, Danny gradually applied his body weight until he was standing upright. Part one was successful. He was upright without the floorboards creaking to alert anyone downstairs, part two would be tricky getting down the old stairs without a sound. Listening as he edged onto the landing, he rolled his feet slowly from heel to toe as he went.

Danny froze at a faint sound from somewhere at the back of the house. He considered jumping the stairs to the hall below, but in the darkness, he thought better of it. He'd probably break his ankle or rupture something in his healing stomach and be doubled-up in pain. Instead, he moved down the stairs, knees bent, using the muscles in his legs to move his body weight smoothly from foot to foot. Halfway down, a creaking wooden step broke the silence. Time, and Danny, stood still as he froze and listened. A noise came from the kitchen, and a split second later, Danny jumped the last of the steps. He ignored the pain in his shoulder as he bounced off the hall wall at the bottom of the stairs and ran for the kitchen with his Glock ahead of him. Just before he got to the kitchen door, he could feel the air pressure in the house change as the back door opened and bodies moved out. Bursting through, Danny's focus darted from the still-swinging back door to Simon's file sitting open on the table next to his mobile phone. Danny came to a halt, his bare feet gripping the vinyl floor-ing, before he exploded into a sprint back towards the front door.

'Fuck's sake, come on,' he yelled in frustration, losing valuable seconds fumbling with the door chain and latch.

The door smacked loudly into the wall as Danny yanked it open and ran out into the street, swinging his gun in front of him as the sights and his eye line moved as one. Twenty-five metres up the road, two men jumped into the back of a Nissan Qashqai, its engine and lights already on as it waited for them. Danny reacted instinctively, sprinting after it, his legs and arms pumping as fast as they could while his head remained still, his eyes locked and focused on the number plate as the car sped away, the two men pulling the doors shut while it moved. Danny padded to a halt. Great clouds of breath billowed into the night air as he drew cold air into his burning lungs and breathed hot air out. He repeated the registration plate over and over in his mind before turning to walk back towards his house. Returning from his night shift, Danny's neighbour, Mr Robinson, got out of his car. His mouth opened as he stared at Danny walking towards him in his underpants, holding a Glock 17 handgun.

'Morning,' Danny said, giving him a nod as he turned down the path and went inside, slamming the front door shut behind him.

'Bloody weirdo,' Mr Robinson muttered under his breath.

Inside, Danny walked into the kitchen, turning on all the lights as he went. He shut the back door, put the gun down on the table next to the open file, and flicked the kettle on.

No chance of sleeping now.

He looked at the picture of Snipe looking back at him, then closed it and wrote the registration plate and silver Nissan Qashqai on the front of the file. As he looked at it, a nagging thought bounced around in his head. He made a coffee and ran through the events of yesterday until he came to the point where he'd gone to the kerb after Simon and his men left. A silver Nissan had been parked at the very top of the road, too far to get any detail, but it had four people in it. He remembered the hairs on the back of his neck had been up, and he had the weird feeling he was being watched.

So who the hell are you guys?

By the time Simon's car turned up at 8.00 a.m., Danny had studied the file back to front, showered, shaved, and eaten breakfast. He looked out the window as the driver got out, smiling to himself at the familiar face of his old friend, Thomas Trent.

'Danny, good to see you, mate,' Tom said when Danny opened the door.

'You too. It's been a while. You've put on a few pounds,' Danny said with a grin.

'Mmm, yeah, that's what two years behind a desk will do. I still look better than you,' he said, looking at Danny's tired face and the way he winced at putting his jacket over his freshly bruised shoulder from jumping down the stairs.

'I won't argue about that. It's a long story. I'll tell you on the way,' Danny said, sliding his Glock into a shoulder holster before picking up the file and following Tom to the car.

'You got a licence for that?' Tom said, pointing at the gun.

'No, what? You going to arrest me?' Danny said, getting in.

'Not me, mate, I've seen nothing,' Tom said, driving the car away from the kerb.

CHAPTER 31

After clearing security and checking his gun in before he could enter, Danny reluctantly took the lift with Tom to the fifth floor. They stepped out and headed down the corridor to one of the Secret Intelligence Service building's larger incident rooms.

It was a hive of activity, with over twenty agents working hard at workstations and on their phones. At the front of the room, the familiar figures of Edward Jenkins, Simon, and Simon's predecessor, Howard—his code name dropped when he moved out of the shadows to become the Minister for Defence—using his real name, David Tremain. They turned as he marched through the room towards them, their faces changing from a greeting smile to puzzlement at Danny's dark frown and gritted teeth. Before anyone could say anything, Danny slapped the Project Jericho file down onto a table and powered a left hook into the side of David Tremain's face, sending him crashing to the ground. In the blink of an eye, his security detail had their guns drawn and pointing at Danny's head.

'That's for Project Jericho, you bastard,' Danny said,

picking the file back up and waving it at David. 'You've been pulling my strings from the start, from army selection to Afghanistan, to using me for your government experiments in Project Jericho. I always wondered why me, why you always turned up at that key moment, from the Volkovs to Buster Merridew to General McManus.'

'It's alright, put the guns away,' David said, waving his men away as Simon and Edward helped him up. 'I'll let you have that one. I deserve it, but you have to understand the circumstances of the times. The government discovered the Russians and the Chinese were running similar projects. The threat of war against genetically engineered super soldiers was too great to ignore. Personal ethics didn't come into it. We all follow orders, Daniel, and we all have our superiors. The projects all failed, the Russians and the Chinese all suffered losses, as did Jericho. You were the only success. You were too valuable to wander off into civvy street.'

'The only success! What about the failures? You created a monster in Snipe. All the innocent people he's killed, that's on you,' Danny shouted back.

'Many things are on me, Daniel, I make decisions I have to live with every day. But what I do, I do for my country and would do it all again,' David answered back, unrepentant.

The two men stared at each other until Edward stepped between them. 'Come on, this is getting us nowhere, we have more urgent things to deal with,' he said, leading Danny over to the interactive screens full of the latest information on Snipe's movements.

'Here, get this checked out. Nissan Qashqai, silver,' Danny said, showing Edward the number plate and description written on the back of the file.

'What's this?'

'It was outside my house when Simon called yesterday, and whoever was in it broke into my house at three this morning.'

'Do you know what they were after?' Edward said, clicking his fingers at one of the agents at a desk nearby.

'No, but they had a good look at this file. If I were to guess, I'd say we're not the only ones looking for Snipe.'

'Yes sir,' said the agent.

'Run a check on this vehicle. Also, put in a call to traffic. I want all CCTV and number plate recognition hits for the last two days.'

'Yes sir,' the agent said, turning back to his monitor.

'Did you see who was in it?'

'Not up close. Dark hair, tanned skin. Maybe Turkish or Egyptian, Middle Eastern in appearance,' Danny said, looking at the screens.

'Middle Eastern? Come and look at this,' Edward said, taking Danny to one of the big interactive screens at the side of the room.

An aerial shot from a drone showed a burnt-out garage workshop in the centre of the screen, arrows banded out to show the burned up bodies of Marco Binelli, his father, and the two mechanics. Below them were the two named bodies of the police officers.

'I saw that on the news. What's the connection?'

'Marco Binelli was a close friend of Nicholas Snipe's brother, Terrence Snipe; he even visited him in prison,' Edward said, tapping a mug shot of Marco from a run-in with the police a few years ago.

'Do you think Snipe killed them all?'

'No, we have a witness who saw four Middle Eastern-looking men speeding away in a BMW moments before the garage went up.'

'Four Middle Eastern men. So who the fuck are these guys?' Danny said, thinking out loud.

'Iranian Secret Service,' came Simon's voice from behind them.

'Iranian?' Danny said in surprise.

'Yes, the fellow Snipe acquired the case from was Alboraz Hosseini, an Iranian scientist trying to sell state secrets for money and a new identity. As one would imagine, the Iranian authorities are rather desperate to get them back,' Simon said, stepping to another screen to tap the picture of the dead Iranian.

'What kind of state secrets?' Danny said, pushing Simon further.

'Ah well, those naughty Iranians have been breaking the terms of their nuclear capability sanctions by developing a rather advanced compact nuclear weapon, the plans of which are locked in a metal case that's in the possession of our friend, Mr Snipe. If these plans become public knowledge, Iran could see the world powers taking military action like they did in the Iraq war over Saddam's alleged weapons of mass destruction. Hence, the case is a matter of top priority. We can not have it falling into the wrong hands.'

Danny was about to tell Simon where he could shove his case when an agent gave a shout that news was coming. The screen to his left flicked on to an Indian newsfeed showing the blood-stained apartment of a murdered family and a body found in the slums.

'Who's this?' Edward shouted over multiple conversations.

'Dr Vihaan Kapur, murdered at his home in Mumbai yesterday evening,' came a voice from behind a computer monitor.

'Who's the other guy in the slums?' Danny said, trying

to make sense of the report. When he turned, he caught Simon giving a look to David across the room.

'No bullshit. Who's the other guy?' Danny growled at Simon.

'He's one of ours, an asset, code name The Hawk. We sent him after Snipe.'

'Any other little nuggets of information you'd like to share with the class?' Danny said, frowning at Simon. When he didn't answer, Danny turned back to the screens. 'So we know he was in Mumbai last night. Where's he been?'

Edward brought up a new page of information on the interactive screen in front of them.

'Monday the third was the first kill, Hosseini in Istanbul. Ten days later, he's in the UK and kills the man in charge of Project Jericho, General Neil Cracknell. I think we can assume he went to see Marco Binelli in Shadwell somewhere in between, which is why the Iranians killed him.' Edward dragged the information into date order before continuing.

'Let's see, Monday seventeenth, Snipe kills Dr Heinrich Mann in Stuttgart, Germany, and yesterday he kills Dr Kapur in Mumbai, India.'

'Sir.'

'Yes Benson,' Edward said to one of his agents making his way across the room towards them.

'Nicholas Snipe was back in London in between Stuttgart and Mumbai. He went berserk on an underground Tube on the morning of the twenty-first. Here, I've pulled the CCTV footage from the transport police,' said Benson, tapping the interactive screen to bring up the footage of Snipe from when he was seated, to wiping Baz and his friends out before walking off the train and out of the station.

'Where is this?' Danny said at the point just before Snipe pulled his hoodie and cap back on, giving a clear view of his clean-shaven face and blonde crew cut.

'The District line. He got off at Whitechapel underground station.'

'Whitechapel, that's just above Shadwell, isn't it? Near Binelli's garage. He's returning to the same area. Why?' Danny said, looking at the screen.

'Benson, get on it. Past addresses for Snipe and his brother. Check out any friends or family in the area,' Edward said.

'Yes sir,' Benson replied before heading back to his desk.

'Where's he going next? Who's left from Jericho?'

'Lieutenant Thomas and Sergeant Burns are here in London at one of our safe houses. We've got a team babysitting them. That just leaves Dr Samantha Mandrell in Cape Town. We have the other possible targets covered.'

'Other targets?' Danny said, looking at Edward.

'Our Minister for Defence Mr Tremain over there for one. He was ultimately in charge of the entire project. Then there's Simon. He was Snipe's handler after he came out of a coma. Then there's you.'

Danny looked from Edward to Tremain to Simon, deep in thought.

'Have you warned Dr Mandrell or the South African authorities that she's in danger?'

'What? Announce that one of our government agents has gone rogue and that he's out to kill a doctor we had carry out genetic experiments on him? Come now, Daniel, you're not that naïve,' Simon said sarcastically.

'Get me Tom and two men of his choice on the next plane for Cape Town,' Danny said, ignoring Simon's comment and turning to Edward.

'Ok, will do,' Edward said, walking off to arrange it.

'I have a contact in Cape Town. Call him as soon as you get there. He'll supply you with weapons,' Simon said, pausing to get Danny's full attention. 'But Daniel?'

'What?' Danny said impatiently.

'You do not make contact with Dr Mandrell. Just watch her. She's the bait to trap Snipe. If he turns up there, you capture him and find out where the case is. By any means, do you understand? We must have that case. You do not kill him, not until we have it.'

Danny maintained eye contact with Simon, his look not hiding his disdain for the government man. Eventually, he gave a small nod and walked off to talk to Tom.

CHAPTER 32

Two miles away from the Secret Intelligence Service building, an 'Ed's Carpet Fitter' van sat parked up in a side street. Babak sat in the front passenger seat with a laptop open on his lap, its volume up full, as Darius, Kaveh and Farid leaned in from the driver's seat and back of the van to listen. They'd hacked Danny's phone when they broke into his house, allowing them to follow its whereabouts and access its microphone and camera undetected any time they wanted.

'I can't believe they're lying to their own men about the contents of the case,' Farid said, shaking his head.

'They are snakes, brother, they lie to everyone,' Kaveh said back to him.

'Shhh, quiet,' Darius snapped, silencing them instantly.

"Get me Tom and two men of his choice on the next plane for Cape Town."

Babak disconnected the call when the conversation in the meeting room ended, leaving the van in silence while they all waited for Darius to decide upon the next move.

'We follow Pearson. If he is as good as they say, he will lead us to Nicholas Snipe. We will go to Cape Town.'

There was a groan from behind them, causing them to turn slowly. Ed the carpet fitter's eyes rolled around in his head as he came round. An egg-sized bump on the side of his head throbbed painfully from where Babak had knocked him unconscious with a tyre wrench. Farid and Kaveh both jumped on him, taking turns to punch him in the face until he stopped moving.

'Is he out?' Darius said, his eyes never leaving the pictures taken from Simon's file showing Dr Samantha Mandrell's information.

'He's out.'

'Good, then we go. We have work to do.'

CHAPTER 33

After killing Dr Vihaan Kapur, Snipe had gone straight to the airport. Wearing a shoulder-length mousy brown wig, brown contact lenses and a moustache, he boarded an Ethiopian Airways plane on a South African passport and flew to Johannesburg. After a five-hour wait, he caught a FlySafair Airlines flight to George City, South Africa, and headed for the city's bus depot. He removed his disguise in the terminal toilets and yawned as he boarded a bus for the six-hour journey to Cape Town. After showing the ticket to the driver, he headed towards the back of the bus. His brother was already sitting in the window seat, so he sat with him next to the aisle. He shoved his rucksack down by his feet and put the seat back, pulling his baseball cap down over his eyes before attempting to go to sleep.

'Fucking six hours on this stinking shithole of a bus, thanks, bruv. Why couldn't we just fly to Cape Town, eh? We could have been drinking beers in a five-star hotel by now,' came the voice of his dead brother rattling around in his head.

'I told you, Tel, I can't risk the airport in Cape Town. After the general and the two doctors, they will almost certainly have people watching the airport and Dr Mandrell,' he said, lifting his cap to look at Terry sitting next to him.

The man in front turned to look back between the seats, frowning at Snipe talking to himself while looking at an empty seat.

'What the fuck are you looking at, you bug-eyed wanker. Go on, turn your head, fuck off,' Snipe growled, leaning forward to look at him menacingly.

The man quickly turned away, leaving Snipe to lean back, pull his cap down, and go to sleep as the bus rumbled out of the station.

'You said they'd be watching the doctor, so how do you plan on getting to her?'

'One thing at a time, Tel. I'll deal with that when I get there. Now do me a favour, shut the fuck up so I can get some sleep.'

CHAPTER 34

Danny and Tom walked into the arrivals hall at Cape Town International Airport. Two of Tom's trusted teammates, Malcolm Lamb and Ian Gibbs, followed close behind. They headed straight to the Budget car rental desk, where Tom filled out the paperwork and paid for two hire cars. As they were on MI6's expenses, Danny booked them all into the five-star Marriott Hotel Crystal Towers, which they checked in to and dumped their bags in before meeting up in the foyer.

'Ok, you two go to the Neuroscience Institute at the University of Cape Town, find Dr Mandrell and keep an eye on her. Me and Tom are going to see Simon's contact to get some firepower. We'll be with you as soon as possible,' Danny said, unlocking his rental car door.

'Got it,' Malcolm said, moving to their car.

'Just keep her under surveillance, ok?'

'Ok.'

'Lads,' Danny said, stopping him and Ian as they were about to get in their rental car.

'Yeah,' they both said at the same time.

'If you see Snipe, you call me, ok? No heroics. You're unarmed, and he's more deadly than you can imagine.'

'Got it,' Malcolm said, nodding before shutting the car door.

Danny watched them go, then got in the other car with Tom.

'Don't worry about them. They're good men, the best. Anyway, Snipe might be a no-show. He's got to know we'll be after him,' Tom said, driving out of the airport.

'He's coming. I can feel it,' Danny muttered, punching the number into his phone for Simon's contact, Malaki.

'Heita,' came the South African slang for hello in an equally thick South African accent.

'Malaki?' Danny said

'Who's asking?'

'The man from London in the expensive suit said you'd be able to provide us with some equipment for our hunting trip?'

'I'll text you the address. Be there in half an hour.'

The line went dead before Danny could answer, a ping sounding twenty seconds later as the address came in.

'Kingdom Hall of Jehovah's Witnesses, Comet Drive, Ikwezi Park. You've gotta be shitting me,' Danny said, putting the address into the map on his phone.

'That's not going to help. I think we're well beyond redemption, mate,' Tom said with a smile as he turned out of the airport onto the dual carriageway, heading towards Ikwezi Park.

———

They arrived twenty-five minutes later, pulling into an estate of single-storey, brick-built homes, with dry scrub yards, some with walled-in gardens, some without. The church was in the middle, its car park empty, and the place looking closed.

'Great, what do we do now?' Danny said, the heat and flies making him irritable as both flooded in when he put the window down to look around.

'Heads up, over there,' Tom said, nodding over to the walled-in house opposite the church. A man looked nervously up and down the road while leaning out from a heavy metal gate.

Satisfied that no one else was around, the scruffy-looking black guy in a dirty T-shirt with holes in it beckoned them over.

'Fuck's sake, he looks like a bloody tramp. I hope his guns look better than he does,' Danny grumbled as they exited the car and walked across to the guy. 'You Malaki?'

'Yeah, quick, come in, come in.'

They followed him in, waiting while he slid three heavy metal bolts across the back of the gate to lock it shut.

'Rough neighbourhood?' Danny said, his eyebrows raised.

'Not for me, but you two wouldn't wanna be here after dark. Come this way,' Malaki said with a big grin.

He led them around to the side of the house. Between it and the six-foot wall topped with cemented-in broken bottles, stood an old and rusty shipping container. Malaki unlocked a heavy padlock on the door latches and pulled it open. He turned on the light inside, and they stepped inside what looked like a normal workshop with benches along the sides and tools hanging on the walls. A heavy metal topped workbench sat in the middle. As Danny and Tom stood next to it, Malaki pulled the door shut and joined them.

'Well, have you got something for us or not?' Danny said, looking around and not liking what he saw.

'You got the money?'

Danny reached inside his jacket and pulled out a big wad of rand notes to show Malaki.

'Ok, then I've got something to show you,' Malaki said, reaching under the workbench.

He pressed a release button, making the section of floor under the bench pop up a few centimetres. With a gentle push, Malaki slid the bench and section of floor back to reveal steps going down into another container buried underneath them.

'Careful as you come down,' Malaki said, leading the way.

They followed him down, looking in amazement at every wall covered in handguns, machine guns, rifles, and even a few rocket launchers, grenades, and plastic explosives.

'So what can I tempt you with?' Malaki said, still grinning.

'Bloody hell, you've got enough in here to start a small war,' Tom said, picking up and inspecting a Smith & Wesson M&P9 handgun.

'I'll take four Glock 17s, spare magazines, and four boxes of ammunition,' Danny said.

'Good choice,' Malaki said, fetching the guns off the rack.

'You got any shoulder holsters?'

'Yes sir, anything else?'

'We'll take the radios,' Danny added, spotting a row of long range two-way radios with tiny earpieces and clip mics.

'Is that your lot?'

'Yes, that's it.'

'Ok, let's do the deal,' Malaki said, grinning.

They paid him without quibbling on the price and left

with the guns and ammunition in a supermarket carrier bag. Malaki slammed the gate behind them, locking it the second they were outside.

'Let's get out of here,' Danny said, suddenly feeling very self-conscious standing out in the open with a bag of illegal firearms.

'My thoughts exactly,' Tom said, climbing into the rental car and spinning it around on the dusty scrub, before heading back the way they came.

CHAPTER 35

Further up the road, tucked in behind a beaten-up seven-and-half-tonne flatbed truck, Darius and the others slid up in their seats and leaned to the side to see the rear of Danny's rental car disappearing in a cloud of dust.

'Do you want me to follow?' said Babak.

'No, we know where they are going,' Darius said, closing the laptop they'd been listening to Danny's hacked mobile on.

'So what do you want to do?' Farid said from the back seat.

'This man Malaki has guns; Pearson and his men have guns. We couldn't get any through airport security, so we need guns,' Darius said, pointing at Malaki's metal gate.

Malaki had just finished locking up the container when someone banged on the heavy metal gate, slapping their palm on it several times to make a loud, booming sound. Immediately on edge, Malaki lifted the back of his shirt and placed a hand on the gun in a holster attached to the side of his belt. He'd already had two visits this morning, the two men sent by the man in London and one from an old contact, a big man with intense blue eyes and a specific list of items he wanted. A third visitor could only mean trouble.

'Who's there?' he shouted, the noise of a large diesel engine revving somewhere close by, making it difficult to hear.

A murmuring came back, too quiet to understand. With his gun by the hatch, Malaki opened the metal spy hole in the centre of the gate to look out. A diesel engine screamed, and all he could see was the JAC Motors logo on the front of the truck hurtling towards him. Before he could get out of the way, it struck the gate, ripping it out of its fixings, carrying it and Malaki back until all three thudded into the brickwork of the house. A cloud of flying masonry and brick dust engulfed the front of the truck. There was a crunch of gears as it settled, then a screech as Kaveh pulled the truck out of the debris and manoeuvred it across the hole in the wall, keeping the damage out of sight from anyone passing by.

Babak and Farid grabbed either side of the buckled-up gate and pulled it back, letting it clang to the ground on the dirt drive behind them. Malaki lay behind it, broken. He wheezed, and blood trickled from his mouth and nose. The money Danny had paid him had come out of his pocket and fluttered in the dirt all around him. Unable to move or talk, Malaki's eyes followed Darius as he walked up to him and dropped onto his haunches. He searched through Malaki's pockets and pulled out the key for the container.

'Thank you, my friend,' he said with a smile before popping upright and walking off.

Farid followed Darius, while Babak came towards Malaki. He watched helplessly as Babak picked up a metal re-enforcement bar from the rubble. As Babak raised it above his head, all Malaki could do was watch as he brought it crashing it down on top of his head to put him out of his misery.

When he entered the container, Darius and Farid were tearing the workshop apart.

'I don't understand, there's nothing here,' Farid said, throwing tools onto the floor from the workbench along the side of the container.

'He said, 'careful as you come down',' Babak said.

'What?' Darius said, looking back at him.

'On the phone, before they picked up the guns, the man out there said, 'careful as you come down'. Then the audio went crackly.'

Darius looked at the floor around the workbench. A dusty footprint lay on the metal surface. Only half was visible, ending where the next metal floor panel extended away under the bench.

'It's under the bench,' Darius said.

The three men moved over and worked their way around the bench until Babak found the release button. They watched the bench pop up a few centimetres, then they slid it forward and made their way down the stairs into Malaki's armoury.

'Take a handgun each, two assault rifles, and ammunition. Hurry. We need to go, we've been here too long already,' Darius said, looking at his watch.

CHAPTER 36

Danny and Tom entered the car park at The Neuroscience Institute at the University of Cape Town. They sat in the car while Tom called Malcolm Lamb.

'Hello.'

'We're in the car park. Where are you?'

'In the cafeteria, watching Dr Mandrell drink coffee and eat something almost resembling a ham sandwich,' Malcolm said, relaxed and upbeat.

'Is it busy?'

'Yeah, there are students all over the place. I feel like the oldest one in here.'

'Good, you and Ian haul your old asses out to the car park. We've got the guns and some radios for you. She'll be safe enough there for a bit,' Tom said, while Danny stood by the car, his eyes scanning the car park for any sign of Snipe.

'Ok boss, on our way.'

Tom hung up and got out of the car to stand by Danny.

'I can't see him turning up here. Can you?'

'Unlikely, too many people. If he comes here at all; he'll probably come for her at her home at night,' Danny replied.

'There goes sleeping in that king-sized bed tonight,' said Tom, waving Ian and Malcolm over to the car.

'Yep, we'll watch the house, both cars on either end of the street. One in each car sleeps while the other watches. We can split the day into two shifts, a team here while the others get some rest back at the hotel,' Danny said, relaxing a little at the unlikely prospect of Snipe attacking Dr Mandrell in broad daylight in a packed university.

'Boss, Danny, here you go,' Malcolm said, handing them a takeout coffee cup each.

'Thanks, mate. Guns and radios are in the boot. Be discreet, guys,' Danny said, taking the coffee while the two of them opened the boot.

They slid their jackets off and looked around before putting the shoulder holsters on and sliding their jackets back on. They did another quick check before sliding the guns into the holsters and hooking up the radios, mics, and earpieces.

'What channel are we on?' Ian asked, slamming the boot shut.

'Eighteen,' Danny said.

Ian and Malcolm turned the radios on and turned them to channel eighteen.

'Soundcheck, one, two,' Malcom said.

'Hearing you loud and clear,' Tom said, speaking normally into the microphone clipped just inside his jacket.

'Ok, you two get back in there. The doctor knows Danny's face, so we'll keep eyes on who comes and goes from the car park.'

'Roger that, boss,' Ian said, walking with Malcolm back towards the university entrance.

The afternoon went by slowly. Danny and Tom sweated in the car with all the windows open as the South African sunshine cooked them slowly. At five past four, Ian's voice came over the radio.

'The doctor's finished for the day. She's heading out the main doors now.'

'Roger that. We have a visual,' Danny said, seeing her step out and walk across the car park towards her car.

Ian and Malcolm appeared a few seconds later and headed for their own rental car. As the doctor pulled out of the car park, Danny and Tom followed at a distance, with Ian and Malcolm falling into line behind them. They drove for twenty minutes, eventually turning into an estate full of neat townhouses. The iconic Table Mountain sat in the distance, supplying a dramatic backdrop to the estate. When the doctor tuned onto her drive, Danny and Tom drove on by while Ian and Malcolm pulled over next to some trees and a bush. Down the road, Danny and Tom turned the car around and headed back.

'Park it on there,' Danny said, pointing to a patch of wasteland with a view of the doctor's house but far enough away to not raise suspicion.

'Ok, settle in, people. It's going to be a long night.'

And it was, apart from a few dog walkers and a brief bit of excitement when a delivery van turned up and sat outside the house. The team was a second away from rushing over when the driver finally got out and shuffled to the door with a parcel under his arm.

At eight the next morning, the doctor came out of the house with a teenage girl in a school uniform. They followed her as she dropped the girl off at school and drove to the university.

Danny and Tom left Ian and Malcolm to do the first shift at the university while they got some sleep at the hotel.

CHAPTER 37

Snipe arrived on the university campus back in disguise in the shoulder-length mousy brown wig, brown contact lenses, and a moustache. He pulled his baseball cap low and pushed the round glasses with the clear glass lenses up his nose. He dressed to blend in, wearing chinos, brown shoes and a plain white shirt, and had a rucksack slung casually over his shoulder. He smiled at the security guard as he entered The Neuroscience Institute, where Dr Mandrell worked as a lecturer. Breaking out of the flow of students, Snipe waited for the lady behind the reception desk to finish talking to another student.

'Good afternoon, Miss, I'm looking for Dr Samantha Mandrell's lecture hall,' Snipe said to the receptionist in an almost perfect South African accent.

'No problem, let's have a look for you,' she smiled, tapping away at the keyboard to bring up the details. 'Ah, yes, here it is. It's on the second floor, lecture room L12. That's up the stairs, turn left and it's the room at the very end of the corridor.'

'Thank you,' Snipe replied, heading off up the stairs.

Snipe spotted Malcolm immediately. He was hovering about in the second-floor corridor, his mouth moving like he was talking to himself. Not looking directly at him, Snipe caught sight of the tiny earpiece in his peripheral vision, its thin wire travelling down Malcolm's neck to disappear under his collar to the radio unit. Malcolm's eyes flicked from person to person as they moved between class-rooms along the corridor. Snipe knew what Malcolm was looking for—a face to match whatever photo they had of him, or the body language of a trained military man: fit physique, confidence, killer's eyes, all the same things that had highlighted Malcolm to him. Snipe walked with relaxed strides, his shoulders rolled forward, taking on the bad posture of a man who spent his days hunched over a desk. He walked straight past Malcolm and entered the lecture room.

It was a large room with a hundred seats banked up in a semicircle to look down at the stage and her. The sight of Dr Mandrell brought back more memories of the facility, crashing through his head like waves. Snipe took a minute to get the anger burning inside in check before moving. He looked around the lecture theatre, picking Ian out as easily as he had Malcolm, seated a couple of rows down from the top tier of seats, his head turning as he assessed potential threats from one student to another, the smallest glimpse of a gun showing when his jacket flapped open a touch. Snipe moved along the row of seats above Ian, taking a seat directly above him. He stared at the earpiece and wire just visible under Ian's hair as it disappeared under his collar.

'Go on, bruv, take the gun out of the bag and do him and her. It'd be easy. You can just walk out while this bunch of arseholes run about screaming.'

'No, I want her alone, so I can watch her suffer,' Snipe

muttered quietly, the image of his dead brother looking back at him from the seat next to Ian's.

'Fucking pussy. If you hadn't noticed, they're on to you, Nicky boy, this wanker and the one outside. Hell, there's probably more of them kicking around here somewhere. You haven't got time to play with your little fucking toys. This could be the only chance you've got. Now do her and do him.'

Snipe looked past Terry and focused on Dr Mandrell as she talked and pointed to the slides, showing graphs and pictures on a big screen. Ian, talking softly into his microphone, caught Snipe's attention, so he leaned forward to listen.

'Shift change, about time. Yeah, I'm looking forward to that hotel bed. See you in a minute.'

Snipe's anger built at the thought of more agents arriving at any second. 'Fuck it. If I can't use it on her, I'm not going to waste it,' Snipe muttered.

Shoving a hand into his rucksack, he pulled out a stubby piece of metal pipe, a loop of steel wire coming out from two small holes drilled in the top of it. Snipe leaned forward and flipped the wire loop over Ian's head. Pulling back on the pipe with one hand so it dug into Ian's neck, Snipe pulled the end of a zip tie that protruded from a hole halfway down with the other. Inside the pipe, the tightened tie locked the trigger of a battery powered compact ratchet into the on position. Its high torque end started turning to pull the loop ever smaller as the steel wire wound around a socket attached to the ratchet. Panicking, Ian shot his hands up, pulling the wire enough to get the fingers of one hand between the wire and his neck. By the time he tried to push it up and off, the loop was too small to get past his chin and was getting smaller by the second. As the surrounding students started to panic and scream, Snipe let the tube go and stood up, pulling his handgun out of the rucksack. His wrist flicked the gun up, putting Dr Mandrell squarely in his sights as she looked up, confused and panicked by the fleeing students.

'See you later, Doc,' Snipe said with a grin, squeezing the trigger twice.

At the same moment, a student jumped up from their seat, catching the two bullets intended for Dr Mandrell in the centre of their back.

'For fuck's sake,' Snipe growled, his eyes burning with rage, searching for Dr Mandrell as the student tumbled lifelessly over the seats towards the stage.

He glimpsed her as she ran through a door to the left of the stage. Snipe left Ian and jumped over the seats, heading toward the stage. He stopped when two armed security guards barrelled through the door Dr Mandrell had just exited through. They moved around the stage like a couple of amateurs, guns up, swinging them around as they looked for the gunman amongst panicking students as they fled for the exits.

Snipe slid the gun back into his rucksack and turned his back on the guards, leaving the lecture theatre amongst the crowd. He turned his head away as Malcolm rushed into the lecture theatre to find out what was going on. Straightening back up, Snipe headed along the corridor to the stairs, heading down them towards the exit. As he turned on the landing to descend the last flight of steps to the reception, Danny and Tom were fighting their way up on the opposite side to him. Without looking directly at him, Snipe watched Danny out of the corner of his eye. Apart from being a little older, he was just as Snipe remembered him. He was alert on a higher level than most people, his movements always fluid, his eyes darting around the crowd, taking in all around him, an A1 predator at the top of the food chain. His focus flicked onto Snipe as they passed on the stairs, locking on for a hundredth of a second before flicking off onto another person.

'Don't worry, pal, you'll be seeing me soon enough,' Snipe muttered, moving into reception.

He looked back before walking out the main doors. Danny was standing on the landing, looking in his direction.

CHAPTER 38

Danny stopped on the landing. Something bothered him. His senses tingled, and the hairs on the back of his neck stood upright.

'What is it?' Tom said, stopping a couple of steps above him, eager to carry on and find out what the source of the panic was.

Turning, Danny looked down into reception, scanning the flow of students as they fled down and out of the main entrance. His eyes fell on the back of a tall man with shoulder-length, mousy brown hair and a faded blue baseball hat on his head. Winding back a minute in his head, Danny recalled a glimpse from under the peak of the hat, brown eyes behind round glasses, and a moustache. He walked with heavy plodding steps, his shoulders rounded, an ordinary guy, unfit, the type of guy who spent most of his time at a desk. So why did it bother him so much? Because he wasn't panicking with everyone else.

The man turned his head back at the entrance doors, the peak of his cap tilting back just for a second to give a clear view of his face. The colour of the eyes might have been different, but the shape as they widened and fixed on Danny with that intense stare was exactly as he remembered it. A flicker of a grin curled up in the corners of his mouth before he turned and disappeared from view outside.

'Snipe,' Danny said, heading back down the stairs as fast as he could against a fresh stream of students.

'What, Snipe?' Tom shouted, rushing after him.

'Hey, watch out,' shouted a man, dropping his books as Danny barged past on his way out the door.

He burst out through the entrance doors, cursing the bright South African sun that temporarily blinded him until his eyes adjusted.

'Danny, wait up, what the fuck's going on?' Tom said, catching up with him.

'He was here, just here. We passed him on the stairs. The fucking tall guy, white shirt, brown wig, moustache, baseball hat. That was him,' Danny shouted, his head tracking from left to right, desperately trying to spot Snipe.

'Yeah, I saw him. It didn't look like Snipe. Are you sure?'

'Yeah, I'm sure. It was him. Shit, the doctor,' Danny said, turning and running back inside, bumping past the man as he picked his books up, knocking them back out of his hands onto the floor again.

'Dude, what the fuck?'

Danny raced up the stairs and along the second-floor corridor, bursting into the lecture theatre, stopping at the top to take in the chaotic scene in front of him. One security guard was trying to resuscitate the shot student near the stage. The other guard and Malcolm were desperately trying to get their fingers on the ratchet in the tube to stop Snipe's device. The wire was now so tight it cut into Ian's fingers, trapped between the wire and his neck on one side.

On the other side of his neck, the wire was cutting through the flesh, threatening to sever his carotid artery. Ian's face was bright red, and his eyes bulged as he panicked and struggled for breath.

'Move back,' Danny shouted, drawing his handgun as he ran over.

Malcolm and the guard jumped back as Danny stood over Ian. He shoved the barrel of the gun over the top of the tube and pulled the trigger; the muzzle flashed and sparks flew as the bullet shattered the ratchet's head, severing the wire before blowing what was left of the ratchet out the bottom of the tube. Ian rolled away, taking huge breaths as his released hand pulled the imbedded wire out of the flesh on his neck.

'Where's the doctor?' Danny said, shooting a look at Malcolm and the security guard.

'She's ok, she's with my colleague just through the stage door, room on the right. Sorry, who are you?' the guard said, seeing Tom appear beside Danny with a gun in his hand and suddenly realising he didn't know who these people were.

'State Security Agency, I'm Agent Logan, and these are my men. Who are you?' Danny said, seizing control.

'Grant, Grant Bovey.'

'Excellent work, Mr Bovey, you secure the lecture theatre while we wait for the police,' Danny said, dismissing Grant and turning to Malcolm as he helped Ian up. 'Agent Smith, you take Agent Jones to the car while me and Agent Barker talk to the doctor.'

Malcolm and Ian took the hint and made their way out of the lecture theatre.

'How long do you think we've got?' Tom whispered as he and Danny went through the door to the side of the stage.

'Before the place is crawling with the police, five minutes, tops.'

'No time for niceties then.'

'Nope,' Danny said, smiling at the security guard who stood facing them, his hand up to stop them from entering the room with Dr Mandrell in.

Before he could ask them who they were, Danny stepped forward and kicked him so hard in the balls that his feet left the ground. He went down and rolled around, groaning while holding his crotch. Danny opened the door to see the doctor sitting nervously in a seat. She looked up, expecting security or police, a puzzled look on her face until recognition kicked in and fear took its place.

'Daniel Pearson? It's been years. Why are you here?' she eventually said, her eyes looking towards the door.

'It's ok, I'm not here to hurt you, I'm here to keep you safe.'

'Safe from who? That madman out there?'

'That madman was Nicholas Snipe. He's completely unstable and has already killed General Cracknell, Dr Mann and Dr Kapur.'

The colour drained from her face as she tried to make sense of what Danny said.

'Killed, why? After all these years. Why now? Why me?' she said, panicking.

'It's a long story, and now is not the time to tell it. Look, the UK government sent us here to stop Snipe and keep you safe,' Danny said, pausing to let the words sink in. 'We need to get you out of here right now.'

'Get me out to go where?'

'Somewhere away from here, somewhere safe, just until we can find and stop Snipe,' Danny said, trying to move her along.

'My home! God, my home, my daughter will be home

from school any minute. I've got to warn her,' she said, her hands shaking as she riffled through her bag to bring out her phone.

She dialled her home number, her eyes welling up as it rang and rang.

'Don't worry, we'll get her. But we need to move now,' Danny said, staring at her until she got the message.

She finally nodded and followed Danny out, shaking when she saw the security guard groaning on the floor outside.

'Dr Mandrell, is there another way out of here, not the main entrance?' Danny said forcefully.

'Er, yes, straight down here. There's a fire door leading out the side of the building, but shouldn't we wait for the police?'

'You remember Nicholas Snipe? What you did to him and me? You remember how good he was back then?

Dr Mandrell looked at Danny for a minute, then nodded.

'Well, now he's even better. The police can't keep you safe. I can,' Danny said, looking her straight in the eye.

'Ok,' she said after a few seconds.

'Good, let's go.'

CHAPTER 39

The second Snipe was out the entrance doors, he took off across the car park, covering the hundred metres between the Neuroscience building and the university's Falmouth building only a few seconds slower than an Olympic athlete. He tucked in around the far corner of the building, breathing heavily. Peeping back at the Neuroscience building, Snipe watched Danny dash out of the building, coming to a stop at the edge of the car par, Danny's eyes looking amongst the cars for him as Tom came out and stood next to Danny. They continued looking for a few more seconds before Danny said something to Tom, and the two turned and ran back inside.

'That's right chum, you run along to see if the doc's ok,' Snipe muttered to himself, pulling the cap, wig, glasses and false moustache off and placing them on the floor. Peeling the shirt off his back, Snipe wiped the sweat off his face with it before rolling his disguise inside it. He pulled a black T-shirt and dark shades out of his bag and put them on before placing the rolled-up shirt back in the bag.

Snipe took the shades back off and looked at his watch.

Pinching the brown contact lenses out, he threw them on the floor before sliding the shades back on.

The cops will be here in a moment. Time to go.

Looking back across the car park, Snipe watched Malcolm and Ian walk briskly out of the Neuroscience building and across the car park to their rental car. Ian held a wedge of blood stained toilet paper to his neck, another wedge wrapped around his cut fingers. Snipe frowned to see he was still alive, his face darkening further at the sight of the university's security opening the door of the car he'd stolen earlier that day, its owner's body still warm in the boot.

'Well done, bruv, if you'd just shot that guy and the woman instead of pissing about with your little toy, we'd be out of here now and on to the next one.'

'Shut the fuck up, Tel, I'm thinking,' Snipe growled at his brother.

'Why don't you make me, little brother,' Terry's image growled back.

A large, long wheelbase FedEx delivery van pulled across Snipe's field of vision and stopped. The driver hopped out and slid the side door open. He picked up a parcel, checked the address, and headed in through the building's main door to deliver it. Hearing sirens in the distance, Snipe moved to the front of the van, looking around it to regain a visual on the Neuroscience building. Danny emerged from around the side of the building with Dr Mandrell and Tom. They hurried to a separate car from the other two and got in.

'Excuse me, sir,' came a friendly voice from behind him.

Snipe turned slowly to look at the FedEx driver, pointing to the driver's door behind him.

'Sorry, me old mate, you go ahead,' Snipe said, a wide grin spreading across his face as he stepped to one side.

As the driver approached, Snipe darted forward, head-butting the guy on the bridge of his nose with tremendous force. The skinny man thudded to the floor, out cold, blood flowing from his destroyed nose. Snipe bent down and picked his keys and FedEx cap up off the floor. He put the cap on and slid the side door open, throwing the unconscious man in and shutting it as he slid across the pile of parcels in the back. Snipe jumped into the cab and started the van's engine. As the sirens got louder, Danny's two rental cars drove past him on their way out of the car park. Crunching the van into gear, Snipe put his foot down and followed them out. What he didn't see was a Toyota Land Cruiser pulling out of the far side of the car park, falling in behind them at a safe distance from Snipe and the two cars. It followed them onto the dual carriageway just as a stream of police cars turned into the university car park.

CHAPTER 40

D anny turned in the seat and looked out the rear window at Ian and Malcolm in the car behind.

'How you holding up, Ian?' he said over the radio, watching Ian throw a thumbs-up.

'It looks worse than it is. I'll live, thanks to you. Another thirty seconds and it would have cut my fingers off and severed the arteries in my neck. What kind of nutcase builds a thing like that? Jesus, and to think he was going to use that on Dr Man—'

Danny turned the volume down as quickly as he could but it was too late to avoid Dr Mandrell hearing and looking like she was about to freak out.

'Look, don't worry, you're safe. We'll go to yours and get your daughter and passports. You can pack a bag, and we'll get you to London. You'll be safe there until we catch Snipe,' Danny said, smiling back at Dr Mandrell, trying to put her at ease.

'London! I can't go to London. What about the author-ities here?'

As Danny listened, a FedEx van speeding down the

outside lane caught his eye. He couldn't make the driver out through the sun reflection in the windscreen glass, but the driver's outline and his sixth sense jangling made him reach for the radio as the van started overtaking Ian and Malcolm in the car behind.

'Ian, the van, get out of there.'

His call was too late. Snipe swerved the van violently into the rear quarter of the rental car, kicking the rear out, which sent the car spinning off the dual carriageway onto the dry scrubland that ran beside it. The car disappeared in a cloud of dirt and dust, leaving the FedEx van closing in on Danny and Tom.

'Tom, step on it, get us off the highway,' Danny shouted, trying the radio again. 'Ian, Malcolm, come in.'

'We're fine. But the car's wrecked. Go, just get out of there. We'll catch up with you later,' Ian said, his voice cracking up towards the end as they drove out of radio range.

'Ok, yes, I'll go to London. Just get my daughter, and we'll go to London,' Dr Mandrell said, speaking quickly as she looked at the carnage behind them and the FedEx van closing in.

'Here he comes,' Tom said, swerving across the lanes to block Snipe from overtaking them.

The powerful van rammed into the back of the rental car, whipping them back into their seats until Tom floored the accelerator and pulled away. Danny lowered the window, twisting around in the seat to slide his torso out. He raised his gun, aiming it at the outline of Snipe driving the van. Fighting to keep his arm steady, Danny squeezed off two shots, but all the bumps and swerving sent the bullets wide to punch two neat holes through the centre of the van's windscreen, missing Snipe by a couple of feet. Pulling back as the screen starred across his vision, Snipe took one hand off the wheel and punched the windscreen repeatedly until it broke up and flapped out of his way, still held together by the laminated layer between the glass. With the glass out of his way, Snipe accelerated after them. Danny couldn't see Snipe's face. His eyes and hair remained hidden behind the shades and cap, but that unmistakable insane grin of his was clear as day, and getting closer by the second.

'Can't this tub of shit go any faster?' Danny shouted back through the window at Tom.

'No, hold on, the turn-off's up ahead,' Tom shouted back.

'Get down,' Danny yelled to Dr Mandrell, sliding back inside as Snipe fired his gun out of the glassless windscreen.

Bullets punched through the rear windscreen, whizzing between Danny and Tom and thumping into the radio and heater controls, glass crystals from the rear windscreen taking a millisecond longer to catch up with the 1000-feet-per-second speed of the bullets before showering the inside of the car.

Danny twisted in his seat just as Tom yanked the steering wheel to turn off the dual carriageway. The tyres squealed and fought for grip as they took the corner way too fast. The car started to slide sideways, only straightening up as the smoking tyres found some grip at the last minute. Snipe took the corner after them. The large van, with its high centre of gravity, leaned precariously until the nearside wheels lifted off the tarmac. Jerking the steering wheel away from the bend, Snipe thumped the wheels back down and flew off the bend. He fought to gain control, snaking across a patch of wasteland before smashing through a fence and skidding to a halt by the loading bay of a disused warehouse.

'Should we go after him?' said Tom, looking in the rear-view mirror.

'No, he'll have to wait. We get the doctor and her daughter safe, then we go after Snipe,' Danny said, looking away from the van to Dr Mandrell lying across the back seat crying.

'It's ok, you can sit up now, he's gone,' Danny said, reaching back to brush glass crystals off her shoulder.

'I don't think Simon will see it that way,' Tom said.

Danny turned away from the doctor to look at him. 'I don't give a fuck how Simon sees it. We get Ian and Malcolm, the doctor and her daughter to safety, no argument.'

'No argument from me,' Tom said, continuing to drive.

CHAPTER 41

'Argh, fuck, fuck, fucking fuck!' Snipe yelled, punching the dash repeatedly until he got his anger under control.

He reached across and grabbed his rucksack from where it had fallen into the footwell. As he straightened up, he looked out the passenger window at the flattened chain-link fence and deep-ploughed tyre tracks behind him. He followed them up to the bend on the slip road. A white Toyota Land Cruiser had pulled up where he'd left the road. From this distance, Snipe couldn't make out specific details of the occupants apart from their tanned skin and short, dark crew cuts.

'Hello, hello, who the fuck are you guys?' he muttered.

As he watched, the driver turned the chunky tyres and drove the 4x4 off the tarmac, heading in his direction.

Exploding into action, Snipe flew out of the driver's door and jumped up onto the loading bay. Without stopping, he ran at the door to one side of the roller shutters. The warehouse had been empty for years and the weather-worn door frame split and shattered under the force of

Snipe's shoulder charge. The door flew open, slamming into the wall as Snipe kept running across the loading bay. He slid to a stop by the doors to the offices, ripping the fire evacuation point map of the building off the wall. After glancing at the map, he headed through the set of double doors into the office block and charged up the stairs. Flattening himself against the wall beside a window, he chanced a quick look down at the loading bay. The Land Cruiser had pulled up behind the FedEx van and four men were out, two with assault rifles and two with handguns. They fanned out and approached the loading bay in an experienced and practiced formation. Snipe immediately recognised two of them as the men he'd seen watching his flat in Shadwell.

'What do you reckon?' Terry said from the other side of the window.

'Mmm. Best guess, Iranians after the nuke,' Snipe muttered before looking down at the map and heading off up the corridor.

'There's only four of them, take 'em out.'

'Nah, Tel, I've got a better idea.'

CHAPTER 42

Darius and the others climbed out of the Land Cruiser, taking cover behind the FedEx van. Darius signalled for Kaveh and Farid to head for the open door on the loading bay while he and Babak covered them. Kaveh took the lead, looking along his assault rifle's sight as he swung from the door to the office windows above, looking for threats. Farid stuck close behind him, covering the door as Kaveh climbed onto the loading bay and approached it.

Darius watched their progress, his eyes darting from window to window. Babak knelt at the front of the van with the other assault rifle, ready to spray the area with covering fire if Snipe started shooting. After Kaveh and Farid entered the building and yelled 'clear,' Darius and Babak started moving across to join them. Looking at the office windows above the loading bay, Darius caught a glimpse of Snipe moving away from a window on the first-floor stairwell.

'He's on the first floor,' he shouted, rushing past Kaveh to take the lead as he headed for the stairs.

They worked their way up, keeping close to the wall to stop Snipe from picking them off from above. No one spoke as they reached the first floor and started working their way down the corridor. All communication took place through hand signals as they swept into each room, checking that it was clear before moving on to the next.

Kaveh and Farid entered a large derelict office, stepping around fallen ceiling tiles as they reached the middle of the room. Darius came in next, followed by Babak. They'd only taken a few paces inside when a metallic creak and pop sounded from above. Before they had a chance to turn, Snipe dropped off the top of a ventilation duct above them. He landed squarely on his feet behind Babak, grabbing his shoulder with one hand while shoving the muzzle of his gun into the back of Babak's neck. Darius, Kaveh, and Farid all whipped around, trying to get a lock on Snipe as he tucked in tight behind Babak. Only one of his bright blue eyes was visible at a time as he peeped out from one side of Babak's head, then the other.

'Take it easy, Mr Snipe, let him go and we won't kill you,' Darius said calmly, his eyes focused along the sights of his gun.

A deep, gravelly chuckle came from behind Babak. Snipe's hand disappeared off his shoulder, reappearing a couple of seconds later with a hand grenade in it. Snipe put the ring in his mouth and pulled the pin out, spitting it on the floor.

'Now, let's start this again, shall we, chum? How about you take it easy, or I'll put a bullet in your mate's head and blow us all to kingdom come. Now lower your weapons.'

Darius and the others didn't move. The tension in the room was building with every second.

'I'm not kidding, guys. My trigger finger's getting awfully twitchy and I'm itching to drop this grenade. Now

173

lower your guns, and if you're thinking of spinning me that bollocks about not being afraid of dying, don't bother. Because you don't look that religious, and Allah ain't fucking listening.'

Everyone stayed exactly where they were for another thirty seconds until Darius put his hand up and lowered it, along with his gun. Kaveh and Farid followed his command.

'What do you want, Mr Snipe?' Darius said as Snipe moved out to the side of Babak.

Snipe stood with one arm outstretched, his gun still on Babak's neck, the other arm outstretched, holding the hand grenade. 'You're Iranian right? Sent to get the nuke back?' Snipe said, with a big grin on his face, his eyes wide with excitement, darting from one man to the other, daring them to raise their guns.

'Yes, we're Iranian, and yes, we just want the case back. If you give it to us, we will leave. We have no interest in you or your campaign.'

'What's your name?'

'Darius Klek.'

'What are you, military? Government? Private contractors?'

'Iranian Secret Service,' Darius said, speaking calmly.

'Mmm, well here's the thing, Darius, me old mate. The nuke's safely tucked away somewhere in London. It's armed, and I've been resetting the timer every twenty-four hours. Now, if I'm not around to send tomorrow's reset command, London goes bye-bye. The next thing that happens is the UK government lifts the lid on the knowledge that it was an Iranian nuke, and the world goes to war on Iran. So, if you kill me, you won't have a home to go back to,' Snipe said, his eyes flicking to the image of Terry, smiling as he leaned against the back wall with his arms crossed.

Sure that Darius got the point, Snipe moved his gun off Babak's neck and lowered it before tucking it into his waistband. Without taking his eyes off Darius, he lowered himself down onto his haunches and picked the pin to the hand grenade up. Standing, Snipe continued to hold the grenade in one hand and its pin in the other.

'So what do you want? Money? I can get you money,' Darius said, while Babak edged away from Snipe to stand next to him.

'Not money. I want justice. If you and your buddies help me get it, I'll give you the case,' Snipe said, moving the pin millimetres from the hole in the grenade. 'Have we got a deal?'

Darius weighed up the situation. He looked around at his men as they nodded back, one after another.

'Yes, Mr Snipe, we have a deal.'

'Oh, there's just one other thing,' Snipe said, sliding the pin back into the grenade.

'Go on,' Darius said warily, his trigger finger tensing on the gun down by his side.

'How did you know where I was?'

'We didn't. We've been tracking Pearson.'

'Pearson? Why Pearson?'

'Our intelligence told us you served with Pearson in the SAS and were both involved in Project Jericho. We thought you might contact him, so put him under surveillance. When a government agent went to see him, we broke in and found a file on you and Project Jericho. We hacked his phone and found out they had assigned him to find you and retrieve the case.'

'Assigned by who?' Snipe growled.

'Your MI6, an agent called Simon, and your Minister for Defence.'

'Howard,' Snipe said, his face darkening. 'Get your shit together, Darius, me old mate. We're going back to London.'

'You don't want to follow Pearson and the doctor?'

'I don't need to. When the time's right, he'll come to me,' Snipe said, turning and walking out of the room.

As Darius and his men followed, Babak went to say something, but Darius put his fingers to his lips and shook his head for Babak to remain quiet. They exited back out of the loading bay door and headed to the Land Cruiser. As they passed the FedEx van, a noise came from inside the back, followed by the side door sliding open to reveal the skinny FedEx man stumbling over the parcels scattered across the floor.

'Heads up,' Snipe shouted, pulling the pin back out and throwing the grenade at the poor guy.

His reflex action made him catch it, opening his hands to see what it was. As his face dropped, it exploded, popping the side panels of the van outwards as it covered the inside of the van with bits of delivery driver and flaming parcels.

'Nice catch,' Snipe chuckled, continuing to walk to the front passenger door of the Land Cruiser. 'Right, you drop me at the coach station, and I'll meet you in London,' he said, climbing in.

'No, we stay with you until this is over,' Darius said, getting into the driver's seat while the others climbed in the back.

'No offence, boys, but the five of us stand out like Michael Jackson at a kids' birthday party. Now, I've got half the world looking for me, so I've got to take the long route home alone. You boys get to London anyway you like, but you ain't coming with me. Got it?'

Darius and Snipe locked eyes in a standoff until Darius finally nodded and started the car, pulling away from the burning FedEx van.

CHAPTER 43

After driving out of range of the radios, Danny called Ian on his mobile while Tom continued to drive to Dr Mandrell's house. He talked for about a minute, then hung up.

'Are they alright?' Tom said, concerned for his men.

'Yeah, the rental company is sending a breakdown truck, and they're waiting for a taxi to take them to the airport. We'll meet them there,' Danny said.

'Hey guys, sorry to break up your little team talk, but can we hurry up? I want to get my daughter before that gun-toting lunatic comes back,' Dr Mandrell said impatiently from the back as she called her house for the tenth time, with no answer.

'Ok, sorry,' Tom said, speeding up.

When they got close to her house, Tom parked a little way up the road. They sat for a minute, looking for signs of anything out of place.

'Come on, come on, what are you waiting for? Let's go, I need to know she's alright.' Dr Mandrell insisted, her voice bordering on hysterical.

'Ok, calm down, take a breath,' Danny said, turning in his seat to reassure her.

After a few deep breaths, she pulled herself together and nodded. Danny nodded back to her, and they got out of the car. Tom went ahead, moving along the front of the neighbour's house before running across to the door on the side of the house leading into the kitchen. He flattened himself against the wall beside it and waited for Danny to join him on the other side of the door. Danny's hand pushed the doctor against the wall behind him.

'On three, one, two, three,' Danny said, pulling the door open for Tom to sweep inside.

Following Tom, with the doctor behind him, Danny moved quickly through the kitchen and lounge, heading for the bedrooms. They moved to either side of the daughter's bedroom door and silently counted to three with hand signals, before bursting in. A teenage girl lay on the bed in just her underwear and a pair of headphones that pumped some obscure band's music out of them. She turned her head and screamed at the two grown men pointing guns in her face.

'Er, sorry, here's your mum, er...' stammered Tom trying to look anywhere but at the girl.

'Yeah, er, it's ok. We're the good guys, we'll, er, be outside. Make it quick. The police could be here any minute looking for you,' Danny said, looking equally awkward as he stared at the wall.

They moved into the lounge and waited while Dr Mandrell explained what had happened, and how they had to pack and go to London for a while until they caught Snipe.

'So, who's going to explain all this to Simon, then? We came here to stake out the doctor without contacting her, and end up with a dead student at the university, a gunfight on a main road, and we lost Snipe. Plus, we're going to turn up at HQ with the doctor and her daughter in tow. Not the cleanest mission I've ever been on,' Tom said, shrugging his shoulders at Danny as they waited.

'Don't worry about Simon. I'll take care of him. This is about revenge for Snipe, which means he'll head straight back to London,' Danny said.

Dr Mandrell came through with a couple of bags packed and a very grumpy, dressed teenage daughter behind her. She glared at Danny and Tom, throwing daggers at both of them with her eyes. They checked the coast was clear before getting into the rental car and heading for the airport. Three police cars passed them when they were a few minutes down the road, lights flashing and sirens wailing as they sped towards the doctor's house.

'How the hell are we going to sort all this out? We've got to come back here to live,' Dr Mandrell said, looking out the back window at the police cars disappearing into the distance.

'We'll sort it all out once you're safe, I promise. Once this is over, I'll make sure you get home safe,' Danny said, giving the best reassuring smile he could.

Stripping the handguns down on the drive to the airport, Danny threw the pieces out of the window at random points so no one could pick them up and reassemble them. With the airport looming in the distance, he got Tom to pull over so he could drop the ejected bullets down a drain. They arrived back at the rental car drop-off point just as Ian and Malcolm's rental car arrived, all smashed up on the back of a low-loader truck.

'That's my deposit fucked then,' Tom said, heading into the office to spend forty minutes filling in accident forms.

Danny and the others went into the airport terminal to meet Ian and Malcolm and to book tickets on the next available flight to the UK. Two hours later, they boarded a British Airways flight to Heathrow, London. Danny sat next to Dr Mandrell and her daughter, while Tom and the others sat in the row behind. He asked the air steward for a glass of water and took two painkillers to take the edge off his injuries.

'What's up with your shoulder?' Dr Mandrell's daughter asked, staring at him as he rubbed it.

'It's nothing, a sports injury,' Danny lied.

'Yeah right, I can see the bullet hole scar under your shirt,' she said, pointing to where Danny's shirt flapped open.

'What's your name?' Danny said, changing the subject.

'Andrea. Yours is Danny, right?'

'Yep,' Danny said, wishing he'd let Tom sit in his seat to avoid the third-degree questioning.

'You got any kids?'

'I did once, a boy, Timothy. He died,' Danny said after a long pause.

The two of them fell quiet for a long time until Andrea spoke.

'I'm sorry. How did he die?'

'It's ok, it was a long time ago. Car accident,' Danny said, turning his head to give her a smile.

'Thank you for keeping my mum safe,' she said, before putting her headphones on and turning back to the TV screen in front of her.

CHAPTER 44

They landed at Heathrow at six a.m. to be met by eight of Edward's MI6 agents as they entered the customs hall. The agents whisked them straight through the airport, avoiding all the security checks, to three unmarked cars parked in between two police cars with armed officers standing guard beside them.

'Dr Mandrell, our agents will take you and your daughter to a safe house. Mr Pearson, if you could go with Agent Jones in the car behind, Mr Jenkins and Simon are expecting you at the SIS building.'

'Are you not coming with us?' the doctor said, looking worried as she hugged Andrea.

'It's ok, don't worry, I'll check in with you as soon as I can. Go with them. You'll be safe, I promise,' Danny said reassuringly.

'What about our bags?'

'Don't worry, we'll collect them for you,' the agent next to her said.

They got in the cars and headed out of the airport in

convoy. Danny watched as the doctor's car and leading police car peeled off and headed away, while his three car convoy headed straight on for central London. He thought of sending Nikki a message before they got to the SIS building but realised his phone was in his rucksack, which was probably being collected at that very moment by an agent.

'Here we go. This is going to be fun,' Danny said, throwing Tom a look as the cars pulled into the SIS building's underground car park.

After being hustled through security, they headed up in the lift to the fifth-floor incident room. Danny was going to argue and take the stairs, but with the agents looking like someone had stolen the jam out of their doughnut, he thought better of it and rode up in the lift with them. They entered the incident room and headed towards Edward at the front of the room. Simon looked over and frowned at Danny while he talked on his phone. It was the first time he'd ever seen Simon rattled.

'Who's the fun sponge talking to?' Danny said to Edward, nodding towards Simon.

'The Director General of the South African Secret Service. They're rather upset about the shooting at one of their universities and about a man answering to your description pretending to be part of the State Security Agency. Not to mention a motorway shootout and car chase through Cape Town. Oh, and I nearly forgot, a dead FedEx delivery driver.'

'Oh, is that all? No wonder he's got a face like a smacked arse. How do they know it was us?' Danny said unsympathetically.

'Cameras at the airport caught you escorting Dr Mandrell and her daughter onto a plane. They tracked all of you down from the passenger list, then pulled your passport details. Next thing we know, the President of South Africa is on the phone with our Prime Minister.'

Danny was about to answer when Simon stormed over.

'Two days. You were in Cape Town for two bloody days. Do you realise the political shitstorm you've caused? What part of 'don't make contact with Dr Mandrell' didn't you understand?' Simon said angrily.

'Snipe was already there when we arrived; he damn near killed Ian before opening fire and fleeing the university. The doctor only survived because a student got in the way. We couldn't just leave her there, so we took her for her own safety. What the hell did you want me to do? Leave her there to explain to the authorities why a chemically enhanced nutjob from an illegal secret British experiment is trying to kill her?' Danny replied in a raised voice. The two men stood a couple of feet apart in an uneasy silence, neither one willing to back down.

'Well, you've blown it now. Snipe got away, and we've got no idea where he or the suitcase is.'

'Fine, I'll go home then. You forget, you arrogant bastard, I'm here because of what you did to me. I don't fucking work for you,' Danny said, turning to storm out of the room.

'Danny, hang on, wait a minute,' Edward said, standing in his way as he tried to defuse the situation.

'What? I don't work for that prick.'

'Just wait, we need your help. We have to find Snipe and quickly. You know him, how he thinks, what he'll do next.'

'You don't need me. You've got enough men, you'll catch him sooner or later, and you've lost a case full of secret papers, so what? The Americans, Germans, bloody Chinese, you've all got top secret plans for some secret weapon or other. Why the hell should I care about it?'

Danny said, sidestepping Edward to continue his way to the door.

'It's not plans,'

'I don't care,' Danny shouted over his shoulder, still heading for the door.

'In the case. It's not plans, the case contains a nuclear bomb powerful enough to flatten the whole of central London,' Edward called after him.

Danny stopped in his tracks, letting the words sink in for a second.

'For fuck's sake, why me?' Danny muttered to himself, shaking his head as he turned and walked back. 'You might have mentioned that little bombshell at the start of all this,' he said, locking eyes with Simon.

'Orders from above, a need-to-know basis. If it got out that we have a lunatic with a nuclear device on the loose, we'd have widespread panic. Not to mention worldwide condemnation over one of our agents going rogue, and the political fallout over Iran breaking its nuclear capability sanctions. Britain cannot afford another weapons of mass destruction fiasco,' Simon said, his voice a lot calmer.

'By orders from above, you mean our Minister for Defence, David Tremain?'

'Yes, I do.'

'Shit, I think I liked him better when he had your job. I guess we'd better find Snipe then,' Danny said, his personal grievances instantly forgotten as he focused on the problem at hand.

'We've put more men on Sergeant Burns and Lieutenant Thomas,' Simon said, moving over to a screen with a picture of the targets and a list of men covering each one beside the picture.

'Snipe knows we've got the doctor. Surely he'll go to ground,' Edward chipped in.

'No way. He's insane. I saw it in his eyes. He's coming after all of us. I know it,' Danny said.

'Or he'll set the nuke off in London and take us all out,' Simon said.

'If he was going to do that, he'd have done it the moment he got back to London,' said Danny, turning when an agent tapped him on the shoulder to hand him his rucksack from the airport.

'Thanks.'

Sliding his hand inside it, Danny took his phone out and turned it on. Seeing a voice message from Nikki, he excused himself and left the room to call her back.

CHAPTER 45

Darius and his men arrived back in London five hours after Danny and the others. They took the train from the airport back to the same Airbnb apartment. Babak rolled the carpet back and lifted the loose floorboard by the window to reveal their weapons stashed between the joists. He took them out and handed them to Farid and Kaveh, while Darius reported to the agency.

'What have you got to report, Klek?' his handler said.

'We have made contact with Snipe,' Darius said in an unemotional tone.

'And the case?'

'He has it hidden somewhere in London.'

'Can't you torture the location out of him?' a slight irritation detected in his handler's voice.

'There's no time. The bomb's armed and the timer is set. He resets it every day remotely. He's professionally trained, insane, and has no fear of dying. I doubt we could get him to talk before time runs out and the bomb goes off. That's if we could get him to talk at all,' Darius said.

'What does he want, money?'

'No, he wants us to help him get revenge. We help him, he gives us the case. What do you want us to do?'

There was a pause while the handler moved the decision up the chain of command.

Another voice came on the phone, presumably the man in charge. 'Do what he wants. Once you have the case, kill him.'

'Affirmative, he had to take a more indirect route, but will be back in London tomorrow. We will make contact with him then,' Darius said, looking at his watch, trying to work out when Snipe would land in London.

'Good, report back to us as soon as you have the case and we will arrange your extraction,' the voice said, hanging up abruptly when he'd finished.

'What did he say?' Babak said, looking across at Darius.

'We do what Snipe wants and get the case.'

'I don't like it. I don't trust this man Snipe. He's crazy, he talks to his dead brother.'

'We don't have to trust him. We get the job done, get the case then kill him.'

Babak nodded, but still didn't look happy about it.

'Farid, where is Pearson?'

'He's left the SIS building.'

'Where's he going?' Darius said, walking over to the table to look at the orange dot heading up Walthamstow High Street on Farid's laptop.

'By the direction, I think he's going home for the night.'

'Did you get anything useful?'

'They were talking about the target Snipe wants us to get for him. Nothing useful though,' Farid said, looking at his scribbled Arabic script notes on a pad beside him.

'Ok, everyone, get some rest, we have a busy day tomorrow.'

CHAPTER 46

Snipe was up early, despite only having four hours' sleep after his journey back to the UK. He used a bit of software and a wire aerial to scan and simulate the key's signal, unlocking the Range Rover before opening the boot. When nobody stirred inside the house, he quickly took the spare tyre out and gently tucked a sports bag into the space, feeding some wires through the drain hole at the bottom tyre well. He got down on the drive and slid under the car. When he'd finished connecting the cables to the car's wiring loom, Snipe stood up and carefully lowered the boot, pushing it down until it clicked. He used the same software to lock the vehicle before carrying the spare wheel away with him, waiting until he'd turned onto St John's Wood Road before dumping the tyre in a hedge.

An hour later, he sat in a corner cafe he'd been in many years before. As he drank tea and munched on bacon rolls, the electric pulses in his brain threw up the memory of a mercenary friend from the past sitting opposite. Paulo

Ramirez, another good man killed by Pearson. Snipe looked down the street at the two flats a fixer called Hamish Campbell used to work out of. Years ago he'd supplied Snipe with false passports and identities along with an assortment of arms and explosives. Snipe remembered the day he and Ramirez sat at that very table watching Pearson and a bunch of MI6 agents arresting Hamish. When he looked at the chair opposite, it wasn't Ramirez who looked back at him, it was his dead brother Terry glaring at him.

'Don't start, it's too early,' Snipe muttered to him.

'Don't fucking start, I know what you're thinking, bruv. Memories, yeah. Fucking Pearson, it's always fucking Pearson,' Terry said angrily.

Snipe closed his eyes tight and muttered, 'You're not here, big brother, you're dead. I'm not crazy.'

'Boo,' his brother said, laughing when he opened them again. 'You don't get rid of me that easily.'

Snipe ignored him and took a swig of tea before devouring the rest of his bacon roll. Time to put the Iranians to work.

'I don't trust those sand-munching bastards,' Terry chipped in from the other side of the table.

'Neither do I, but they have their uses for now,' Snipe muttered, picking up a guitar case by his feet and hooking the strap over his shoulder before leaving the cafe. He turned down the high street and headed for the nearest underground station, turning his pay-as-you-go mobile on to send a short text message to Darius, immediately turning it back off again so it couldn't be traced. Half an hour later, he stepped off the Tube train at Notting Hill Gate station. He slid the ticket he'd bought with the bank card from the old man he'd killed in Graz, Austria, into the barrier, and walked through. He removed his baseball cap and sunglasses just before heading up the steps to street level, looking straight into a CCTV camera ahead of him as he passed underneath it. Let's see how long that takes to reach the fucking spooks.

He headed along the main road for a hundred metres before turning down a pedestrian walkway between an electrical shop and an old picture house, leading through to Uxbridge Street and no CCTV cameras. Darius sat in the driving seat of a BMW X5 parked outside the Eggbreak cafe with the engine running. Snipe walked over to the boot, opened it and put the guitar case inside. Shutting it, he moved to the front passenger door and opened it, staring menacingly at Babak without saying a word, until he relented and climbed out to get in the back. Snipe got into the seat with a grin and a chuckle before turning to Darius.

'Morning, mate. Allah be praised and all that bollocks,' Snipe said, still grinning as he looked across to Darius.

'Please do not mock my religion, Mr Snipe,' Darius said back, his face serious and eyes locking with Snipe's.

'Alright, alright, don't get your hijab in a twist. Are the others in place?'

'Yes, Farid and Kaveh are in place.'

'Good, and Pearson?'

'He is on the move,' Darius said, holding up a mobile with a dot on a map, showing Danny's location.

'And you have the scanner and radios?' Snipe said.

'Yes,' said Babak from the back, holding up one of the long range radios.

'We'd better be on our way, Darius, me old mate. I give it half an hour tops before this place is swarming with counter terrorism officers and MI6 agents.'

With that, Darius pulled away, weaving his way through the back streets, eventually joining the Uxbridge Road in Shepherd's Bush to head away from the centre of London.

CHAPTER 47

'T hat's Simon again,' Tom said, holding up his phone with three missed calls on it.

'Fuck him. He can wait. I promised the doctor I'd look in on her,' Danny replied grumpily.

'What have you got against the man? He's got everyone's best interests at heart.'

'Mmm, easy to say when he hasn't tried to have you killed.'

'What? When? Why?' Tom stammered in surprise.

'A while ago in Australia. Long story, mate, let's just say I'll never play computer games again,' Danny said, managing a grin.

'Ok, ok, I'm not going to ask. Take a right up here. The safe house is up on the left, red door.'

Danny turned, knowing which house was the safe house before he'd seen the colour of the door.

'Jesus, could these guys be any more obvious?' Danny said, spotting the two agents sitting in a black BMW outside the house, black suits, white shirts and black ties.

He could even see the radio earpieces with their wires trailing down their necks and under their collars.

'Fuck me, it's the Men in Black,' Tom said with a chuckle.

'They know we're coming, right? I don't want to get my arse shot off by Agent K.'

'Yeah, they've been briefed.'

Danny pulled up in front of the car, watching the agents tense and slide their hands inside their jackets to have a hand on their guns, only relaxing when they recognised Danny and Tom from their pictures.

'How are they?' Danny said, getting out and walking over to their open window.

'The doctor's on edge, but her daughter seems to be taking the upheaval well. They've been asking for you.'

'Ok thanks, guys, how many are in the house?'

'Two of our guys, one on the front door, one with the doc.'

Danny nodded and headed up the path to the front door, which opened before he got there. The agent closed and bolted it behind them the second they were in.

'Morning, Dr Mandrell, is everything alright for you?' Danny said warmly. Throwing a smile and wink to her daughter Andrea when she looked up, headphones on her head as she played music from her phone, she smiled back before going back to her music.

'Yes, thank you, and call me Samantha. I feel I owe you an apology.'

'An apology for what?' Danny said.

'With the shock of that man trying to kill me and the madness of getting out of the country, I fear I was very rude to you and your men. I know you were only trying to keep me and my daughter safe, and I'm sorry.'

'Don't mention it. You are safe. That's the main thing,

and as soon as we catch Nicholas Snipe, you can go home and forget all about this,' Danny said, blushing a little from the apology.

'But what about the police and the university? I left the scene of a crime and the country, how do I go back to that?' the doctor said, a worried look coming over her face.

'It's ok, it's all been taken care of. The bigwigs have sorted it. There's a cover story being written as we speak. An old psychiatric patient from your days working for the MoD in England formed an unhealthy obsession with you, that kinda thing. Which is not that far from the truth anyway,' said Danny, glancing back at Tom as his phone rang again. This time he answered it.

'Ok good, so are you any closer to catching him?'

Danny was about to answer when Tom tapped him on the shoulder.

'Gotta go. Facial recognition's got a hit on Snipe at Notting Hill Gate station.'

'Sorry, I really have to go, I'll keep you informed, ok,' Danny said to Samantha before turning to follow Tom out the front door.

Seconds later they were both in Danny's powerful BMW M4, speeding off up the road.

CHAPTER 48

S nipe climbed the steps up the four-storey block of flats, the guitar case slung across his back. Darius followed close behind him, carrying a backpack. They reached the fourth floor, taking a quick look up and down the walkway to the flats on either side to check the coast was clear. With no one around, they continued up the stairs to a padlocked door giving access to the roof. Darius pulled a crowbar from the backpack, easily levering the padlock and latch off the old wooden door.

'Ladies first,' Snipe chuckled, stepping onto the roof behind Darius.

The block of flats was the highest building for nearly half a mile in all directions, making Snipe and Darius almost invisible from prying eyes when they lay on their bellies, slightly back from the edge of the roof. Snipe flicked the catches on the guitar case and opened the lid. Pulling the pieces out one after the other, he assembled the Barrett Mk22 sniper rifle in seconds, barely having to look at it. He clicked the sights into place before slotting in a ten-round magazine.

'There you go, mate, you sure you can handle it?' Snipe said, handing him the rifle while still trying to get a rise out of him.

'You better hope so. I might miss and put a bullet through your head,' Darius said, his face serious and voice unemotional.

'That's why I like you so much, Darius, me old mucker. You've got a great sense of humour,' Snipe said, pulling two radios out of the backpack.

He clicked one on and pressed the call button. 'Oi Babycakes, Babushka, whatever your name is, you in position?'

'It's Babak, and yes, we are in position.'

'Anything happening?' Snipe said, squinting to look at the house in the distance.

'Two agents just left the house and drove away. The targets are still inside,' came Babak's voice, clicking off in a crackle of static.

'And the others?'

'There are four agents, as you said there would be, two outside in the car, two inside with the targets.'

'Good, have you got the channel from the scanner?'

'Their radios are on channel fourteen.'

'Ok, sit tight and wait for my mark. I'm on my way over.'

Snipe turned the second radio on and selected channel fourteen, sliding it into his left jacket pocket. 'You got eyes on?' he said, putting the first radio in his right jacket pocket.

'Yes, I can see the two agents in the car, none in the house. They are obviously doing their job and keeping away from the windows. Are you sure we'll have enough time to get out of here before the police seal the area off?'

'Don't you worry about that matey, boy. Right about

now, every spare agent and police officer is scouring the streets of Notting Hill Gate for me. We've got plenty of time. Right, I'm off. Just wait for my mark before you start shooting. Only the agents, as we agreed. The others are mine,' Snipe said, sliding another radio out of the backpack to place it beside Darius before heading down off the roof.

'You'r making a mistake, bruv, you can't trust these slippery fuckers,' Terry's voice drummed around inside Snipe's head.

'They'll do as they're told. As long as I've got that case, they'll do exactly as I say.'

'Yeah, but what happens when you give them what they want?'

'It's all under control, Tel. Now shut up and let me concentrate,' Snipe growled.

He headed along the road towards the target house, nodding across to Kaveh and Farid, who were parked way back from the house in a stolen Peugeot 5008 SUV. Before he got close enough to be seen by the MI6 agents in the car outside the house, Snipe moved out of sight behind a van and pulled the radio out from his right pocket.

'Get yourselves ready, boys, it's showtime,' Snipe said, placing the radio on the floor beside him.

He pulled the second radio out of his left pocket, took a breath, and held it to his ear before pressing the call button.

'Control to XK24, come in XK24,' Snipe said, waiting patiently for a few seconds before the speaker crackled into life.

'This is XK24, go ahead, control.'

'The safe house has been compromised. Evacuate the site immediately. Take the principles mobile and await instruction. I repeat, the safe house is compromised, evacuate site now.'

'Affirmative control, XK24 leaving site now.'

Snipe dropped the radio on the floor and picked up the one for Darius and the others.

'Darius, you're up. Make them count.'

Four hundred metres away on the roof of the block of flats, Darius lay on the flat roof breathing steadily, looking through the sights at the crosshairs sitting at head height on the safe house's front door.

'Targets are about to leave the house,' he said through the headset and mic, as shadows appeared behind the patterned glass in the front door.

He breathed out slowly as the door opened the first few millimetres, reducing any shaking and tension in the muscles. He exhaled all the air in his lungs as the first agent exited the house, leading the two targets down the steps toward an agent holding the car door open for them. Aiming just into his hairline to allow for the inch of bullet to drop from that range, Darius gently squeezed the trigger. A couple of hundred milliseconds later, the bullet struck the agent clean between the eyes, the back of his head ripping apart to send blood and brain matter all over the two targets close behind him.

'Go, go,' Snipe shouted over the radio before dropping it and spinning out from behind the van. Crossing his arms, he gripped his handguns, pulling them from their shoulder holsters under each arm.

Before the targets knew what had happened, Darius dropped the agent bringing up the rear as he left the house. The agent by the car stuck to his training, reaching forward to grab a target and push them into the back of the car.

'Come on, come on,' the driver shouted, revving the

engine, ready to dump the clutch and scream off the moment his colleague got in.

The second the other target was in, the agent turned to get in the open passenger door. His head whipped back before he got there. He dropped like a stone, leaving a cloud of red mist hanging in the air where he'd been.

'Keep down,' the driver yelled, flooring the accelerator as he yanked the steering wheel, launching the car out of its parking place. The open passenger door smashed into the parked car in front of them, shattering the window and sending millions of glass crystal across the inside of the car as the impact slammed it shut.

The car snaked down the road until the driver got it under control, hurtling between the parked cars on either side of the narrow suburban road. A short distance ahead of him, Babak pulled out of his parking place in the BMW X5, stopping diagonally across the road to swing an automatic rifle out of the open driver's window. Stamping on his brakes, the agent driving threw it in reverse and floored it, twisting in his seat to look out of the rear window over the two targets crouched in the back. The gearbox whined as the car flew backwards, the agent looking for a gap to spin the car around so they could get away. Before he found one, he slammed on the brakes. Farid and Kaveh pulled across the road behind him, automatic rifles pointed out the windows in his direction.

'Stay down,' he shouted, pulling his gun out, desperately trying to think of a way out of the situation. 'We'll have to run for the house and hold out until help comes.'

He turned to open the car door, only to see Snipe appear from between the parked cars beside him, both guns raised and locked in his direction. Snipe pulled the triggers on both guns at point blank range, blowing the man's face off before he got his gun up. As he stepped back, Farid and Kaveh pulled the car doors open and aimed their rifles at the two in the back.

'Sergeant Burns, Lieutenant Thomas, it's been a long time. Why don't we have a little reunion party?' Snipe said menacingly.

'Fuck you,' Lieutenant Thomas spat back.

'Take them,' Snipe said, turning and walking away while Kaveh and Farid swung their rifles around and started smashing the butts into the two men from either side of the car. They tried to fight and kick out, but with no leverage and no room to move in the confined space, the blows to the body and face soon broke them down enough for Farid and Kaveh to put hoods over their heads and zip-tie their wrists behind their backs. Dragging them out, they manhandled them into the boot of their car, zip-tying their ankles to their wrists behind their backs when they were in. Seconds later, they reversed, bumping up the kerb before turning the car around and heading away from the house. Fifty metres up the road Babak did the same, pausing only for a few seconds to let Snipe into the passenger side before heading to the flats, where Darius strolled out from the stairwell with the guitar case and backpack over his shoulder.

CHAPTER 49

'Jesus, it looks like a bloody war zone,' Danny said, braking hard as he approached the police cars blocking Notting Hill Gate road. He screeched the car to a halt, panicking a bunch of armed response officers who all pointed their rifles at him.

'You did that on purpose, didn't you?' Tom said from the passenger seat.

Danny gave him a grin, flashing his MI6 ID at the frowning officer. He waited for them to let him through, then drove on towards the Tube station. The area was swarming with police cornering off every road, SWAT teams scouring the Tube station, and government agents orchestrating the search teams.

'Something about this doesn't stack up here,' Danny said, pulling up behind Simon's Range Rover.

'Yeah, I know what you mean, it's like he wanted to be spotted,' Tom replied, getting out of the car.

They walked over to Edward and Simon, both of them with a phone glued to their ear.

'We got anything, Ed?' Danny asked.

'No, nothing, we've got him on the Tube station CCTV and on a traffic camera heading up towards Holland Park Avenue. But he turned left onto Uxbridge Street before he reached it, disappearing into a housing estate with no cameras. We've got everyone on all the cameras surrounding the estate. There's no sign of him as he exited. They're running all number plates entering and exiting the area, but that'll take time. We've got the Met doing house to house in the estate, just in case he's held up somewhere,' Edward said, the tone of his voice telling Danny that Edward thought it was as pointless as he did.

Simon got off the phone and joined them.

'Hell of a turnout,' Danny said to him.

'Given the current threat level, the PM has given me the authority to use any resources I see fit.'

'Yeah, the threat of a nuclear explosion tends to be rather persuasive. You know he's not here, don't you?'

'So it would seem, Daniel, I fear Mr Snipe is playing with us, but why?'

Danny's face dropped as a thought crossed his mind.

'The doctor, he's gone for the doctor. Quick, check on her, now.' Danny said, turning to head for his car.

'Wait, the doctor's fine. I spoke to the protection detail a couple of minutes ago. The extra men we sent are there, and it's all quiet. We've also sent men to Thomas and Burns. They should be there any second,' Edward said. His and Simon's phones rang within a few seconds of each other.

Danny stopped in his tracks and turned back, just in time to see both Simon and Edward's faces drop. They looked at each other knowingly before both ended the call.

'What? What's happened? Has he got to the doctor and her daughter?'

'No, it's Thomas and Burns. The bastard's killed our

agents and taken them. Edward, can you go with Daniel and Tom, check out the safe house and see what you can find out. I'll stand this lot down and meet you at the SIS building later,' Simon said.

Danny drove back through the roadblock and headed across London to the safe house. They parked close to the police cordon, flashing their ID before ducking under the tape strung across the road.

Danny walked towards the house, spotting the two long range radios discarded behind a van as he went. He stood in the road and looked at the bloody scene, starting with the agent lying on the steps by the front door, a CSI team busily erecting a privacy tent around his body, moving down to the second agent at the bottom of the steps, then onto the third agent lying on the pavement surrounded by blood and fragments of glass. Danny turned his head and looked at the dented rear wing of the parked car and the tyre tracks heading down the road. Frowning, he turned his head to look at the car in the middle of the road in the other direction. He walked over to it and looked in at the dead driver, flopped over onto the front passenger seat. Bobbing down on his haunches, Danny picked up one of Snipe's spent bullet casings.

Standing backup, he reached in through the glassless window, and grabbed the gear knob, and clicked it out of gear before pushing it back up again.

'What is it?' Edward said, watching him.

'We've got a big problem.'

'What's that?'

'Snipe's not working alone. Something large took the men out by the house, judging by the entry and exit wounds. I'm guessing a fifty-cal from a sniper rifle.' Danny looked away from the house, scanning the surrounding

205

buildings until his eyes fell on the four-storey block of flats four hundred metres away.

'Over there, the flats, it's the perfect position, easily shot from that range. He got them to leave the house somehow, then the sniper took out the three as they tried to get Thomas and Burns to safety. The driver took off forward, hitting the parked car as he pulled out. I'm guessing Snipe had a car waiting to pull out ahead of him. Our guy follows his training and takes evasive action back that way, where they used a second vehicle to trap him in a kill box. The car's gear stick was in reverse,' Danny said, handing Edward the 9mm bullet casing.

'How many men?' said Edward.

'At least four, probably five or six,' said Tom, agreeing with Danny's logic from his military background.

'You've got one on the roof, the sniper. One or two in each car to block them, and one on foot to take out the driver. Thomas and Burns aren't here, so it would have taken at least two people to manhandle them into the escape vehicle,' said Danny, picturing it in his mind.

'Ok, I'll get the police to knock on doors, see if anyone saw anything,' said Edward, heading off to the officer in charge.

'Who the hell has that lunatic got to help him?' said Tom, looking around at the carnage.

'What has Snipe got that people want?' Danny said, frowning at Tom.

'What, the nuke?'

'What else? This was a professional hit, done by a tight unit of men. Men like the Iranians who broke into my house.'

'You think he's done a deal with the Iranians?' Tom said, surprised.

'I don't know, but it's the only thing I can think of that

makes any sense,' said Danny, sending both men into silence as they looked around and thought about the gravity of Snipe with help and a nuclear weapon.

'I'll let Simon know on the way back to HQ,' Edward said, his phone already to his ear.

CHAPTER 50

After his hood was whisked off, Lieutenant Thomas looked around the derelict warehouse, blinking while his eyes grew accustomed to the light. Babak removed the hood from the sergeant in the chair next to him. The sergeant blinked back at the lieutenant, his muscles flexing as he tried to free himself from the thick cable ties holding him to the chair.

The warehouse had no windows or electric lights. They sat in one of four boxes of light from the occasional clear plastic panels in the corrugated roof high above their heads. Babak walked between the chairs and joined Darius, Farid, and Kaveh, standing barely visible in the shadows just outside the square of light.

'Who the fuck are you bastards?' Thomas shouted defiantly, his military conditioning stopping him from showing any kind of weakness.

Without a word, Darius turned and walked towards the exit. The others followed, all of them disappearing into the darkness with only their footsteps echoing all around until they reappeared in another square of light on the far side of the warehouse, before pushing out the exit door. Snipe watched from the shadows, his eyes twinkling with excitement. He smiled to his dead brother standing behind the sergeant's chair. Snipe stayed in the dark for another five minutes just to mess with his captives' minds, then moved forward slowly until he was on the edge of the square of light. The sun's rays from above washed across his face to give him a ghoulish quality.

'Lieutenant, Sarge, it's been a long time,' Snipe said in a low growl.

'Fuck off, you crazy bastard,' Burns yelled at him, straining against the thick plastic zip ties holding his ankles and wrists to the metal office chair.

Snipe darted forward, his hand grabbing Burn's throat, squeezing it hard as he pushed him, tilting the chair back on two legs.

'Crazy! That's the whole point, Sarge. You were part of Project Jericho. You knew what was going on. I hold you just as responsible as the others,' Snipe yelled, his face inches away from Burns'.

'We were just following orders, you know that,' Thomas yelled across at him.

Snipe released Burns, his chair thumping down on all fours as he gasped for air. Taking a step sideways, Snipe powered a punch to the side of Thomas's face, the blow whipping his head to one side before sending him and the chair crashing over onto the cold concrete floor.

'That's not good enough,' Snipe yelled. 'Sean Walters had a stroke. Aaron Jones jumped off a roof. James Fox set himself on fire. Samuel Hollander jumped in front of a train, three months after the project ended. William Brent blew his brains out on an exercise six months after Jericho ended. David Hurne hung himself eight months later. Me, Nicholas Snipe, died twice, brainwashed by the government, unstable. I talk to my dead brother, for fuck's sake. You're all responsible; you all have to pay.'

'Make them pay, bruv, make them all pay,' Terry said as Snipe walked through his apparition into the shadows, reappearing moments later with a petrol canister.

He spun the lid off and poured the contents all over Lieutenant Thomas as he thrashed around on his side, spitting and shaking the liquid out of his mouth and eyes, desperately trying to break the zip ties holding him to the chair.

'No, stop, leave him alone, you bastard,' Burns yelled, straining to get out.

Snipe hurled the empty canister at Burns, the metal container bouncing loudly off his head.

'No, please, I've got a wife and kids,' Thomas pleaded, choking on the fumes, his eyes wide in panic as Snipe pulled a box of matches out of his pocket.

'At least you've had time with a family. Don't you think I would have liked a family? Do you think James Fox didn't want a family? Before Project Jericho fucked him and he set himself on fire. Well, when you get to hell, you can ask him,' Snipe said, dragging a bunch of matches along the striker strip, the chemically dipped tips flaring to light up Snipe's face in a snapshot picture of insanity. A millisecond later, the fumes rising from Thomas ignited in a flash of blue flame, turning yellow as the vapour burnt off and his petrol soaked body caught light, leaving him screaming and thrashing around on his side.

Snipe's face changed from fury to amusement in a flash. His eyes burned bright with the reflections of the flames.

'Shit, I should have brought some marshmallows,' he chuckled, watching Thomas's movements slow to a halt as he passed away.

Burns shrank into his seat when Snipe tired of the burning corpse and flicked his head across to focus on him.

'Now what are we going to do with you, Sarge?' he said, walking up to him and bobbing down on his haunches.

He moved his hand under the sergeant's seat and flicked a switch, emitting a loud beep.

'Fuck off, you bastard,' Burns shouted in Snipe's face.

'Shhh. If I were you, I'd sit very still. There's a pound of C4 explosive connected to a mercury switch fixed to the underside of your seat. Oh, and there's a pressure pad under your arse. It's very sensitive. You move, sneeze, or try to get out of your seat, and they'll be scraping bits of you off the ceiling,' Snipe said, sliding a pair of side cutters out of his pocket to snip the sergeant's ties from his wrists and ankles. 'Right, I've got places to go and people to see. Sit tight, Sarge, I'll be back later to see if you're still in one piece.'

Snipe backed away into the shadows before turning and walking away, chuckling. Burns sat absolutely still. Free, but not able to get free. A trickle of sweat rolled down his cheek as he watched Snipe walk through the square of light on the other side of the warehouse and disappear out the exit door.

'It's done?' Darius asked.

'Yes mate, I'm going to make the call as soon as we're out of here. You know what to do?'

'Yes, we will deliver the package to the meeting point later,' Darius said, eyeing Snipe cautiously.

Snipe gave him a grin and started walking towards the Peugeot 5008 SUV, just as Farid finished screwing new registration plates on it.

'Mr Snipe.'

'Yeah.'

'Make sure you have the case with you when we get there.'

'Of course, Darius, me old mate, you need to relax a bit,' said Snipe, getting into the car and driving away from the warehouse.

'What do we do?' Babak said to Darius.

'We deliver what he wants and get the case. Then we kill him and go home,' Darius replied, his face emotionless.

'Good, I hate this fucking country,' Babak said, squatting down at the front of the BMW to change the registration plates.

CHAPTER 51

When Danny, Tom, and Edward arrived back at the SIS building, they found the incident room packed with additional manpower. Simon had drafted in every available analyst to trawl through London's thousands of cameras, running checks on every vehicle in and out of Notting Hill Gate to the safe house and surrounding areas.

'What have you got there, Trevor?' said one of Edward's supervisors, the analyst's screen catching his eye as he walked between them.

'Video footage, sir. The recognition software flagged it up as a partial match on Nicholas Snipe. It's from a camera on St John's Wood Road at four fifteen this morning.'

'How partial?'

'20% facial match and a 51% body type match, but it's dark and the angles are bad. You can't really see. Looks like he's holding something big before he throws it in a hedge.'

'Mmm, send someone out to pick whatever it is up, then run the footage through the enhancement program.

We'll come back to it later. Tracking vehicles is the key priority at the moment. Good work, Trevor.'

'Yes sir. Thank you, sir.'

A commotion from the other side of the room made him turn.

'Sir, sir, I've got a match,' came the shout from one of the other data analysts.

The supervisor left Trevor and crossed over to him, checking out the information before moving to the front of the room to where Simon, Edward, and Danny stood.

'Excuse me, sir, we've had a hit on the vehicles.'

'Where?' Simon said, following him to the analyst's desk.

'Ok Keith, tell them what you've found,' the supervisor said, stepping to the side so the analyst could show them the information on the computer screen.

'Here, look. Two cars, a BMW X5 and a Peugeot 5008. They enter Notting Hill Gate on the A4204 approximately twenty minutes before the CCTV sighting of Nicholas Snipe. But they don't appear on any of the cameras on the main road or on Campden Hill Road, which means they must have entered the same housing estate that Nicholas Snipe turned into off the high street. Approximately ten minutes later, the Peugeot 5008 appears on Holland Park Avenue, before turning onto the A3220 and heading north.'

'Heading towards the safe house,' said Simon.

'Yes sir.'

'And the BMW?'

'Ah, that was trickier. They must have taken the back streets, keeping away from the cameras on the main roads. But after much searching, I caught them on a traffic camera near Kensal Green Cemetery.'

'That's what, about two miles from the safe house?' Simon said.

'Correct sir. Two point two miles, to be precise,' said Keith with a certain amount of smugness.

Danny's phone rang as he listened. He glanced at it, hanging up when it displayed no caller ID.

'What do we know about the cars?' Edward said over Keith's shoulder.

'The BMW belongs to a dentist in Lewisham. When I got no answer from his home, I called the dental surgery. Apparently, he's on holiday in Tenerife with the family, so I think it's safe to assume the car has been stolen.'

'And the Peugeot?' Simon said.

'Reported stolen this morning. The owner only noticed when he left for work at eight thirty.'

Danny's phone buzzed in his pocket. He took it out and looked at the message.

"Have you missed me, Danny Boy? Answer your phone."

Just as the words sunk in, it rang with no caller ID again.

'Everyone quiet,' Danny said, failing to get Edward and Simon's attention. 'Shut up, it's him. Snipe,' Danny shouted loudly, putting the room into silence.

'Snipe,' Danny said, answering calmly.

'Danny, me old mate. Well?' came Snipe's gravelly voice.

'Well, what?' Danny answered gruffly.

'Did you miss me? I've missed you. We've got some unfinished business to attend to, you and I.'

'Just say when and where, you sick bastard,' Danny replied through gritted teeth.

'All in good time, but first, listen up. There's an empty

warehouse next to a garage and MOT bay on Armoury Way, Wandsworth. The Lieutenant's a little toasty, but if you hurry, the sarge might still be in one piece, or two, or three.' There was a short chuckle, then the phone went dead.

'We need to get everyone to an empty warehouse next to a garage and MOT bay on Armoury Way. Now. Snipe's got Thomas and Burns there,' Danny said, looking to Edward to organise.

'All of you, go, go, go,' Edward pointed and ordered, sending half a dozen field agents running with Danny towards the door.

'Do not enter the building until tactical response gets there, do you hear me? It's likely to be a trap,' Simon shouted after them.

'Tom, go with Danny and report back to me as soon as you know what's going on,' said Edward, before jumping on the phones with Simon to arrange a tactical response team and police armed response.

Jumping into his BMW M4 parked in the bay next to Simon's Range Rover, Danny reversed out of the parking place and punched it into gear, spinning the tyres on the shiny concrete and shooting out of the SIS building's underground car park behind two MI6 cars. Even with the lights and sirens, the 4.7-mile journey still took nearly ten minutes, the three cars pulling into the empty car park only seconds ahead of the counter terrorism unit and police armed response cars.

'What if he's booby-trapped it with the nuke?' Tom said as they waited for the counter terrorism unit to enter and clear the building.

'Then we can all kiss our arses goodbye, mate. Anyway, I don't think so.'

'I wish I was as sure as you,' Tom said, raising his eyebrows.

'Nah, this is more games. I don't know what he's up to right now, but when he's finished, he wants his one-to-one with me. That much I am sure of.'

'You've beaten him twice already,' Tom said with a half-hearted smile.

'Maybe he's going for third time lucky?' Danny said, rubbing his shoulder.

'The shoulder's still bothering you then?'

'Yeah, it hurts like hell. But the gunshot wound to my stomach's only giving me the occasional stab of excruciating pain, so that's progress,' Danny said with a smile.

As soon as the team leader emerged with his men, Danny headed in their direction.

'Whoa, keep back, I can't let you go in. Lieutenant Thomas is dead, and Sergeant Burns is stuck to a chair rigged with an explosive device. You'll have to wait until the bomb squad gets here to disarm it.'

'Who's in there with him?'

'No one. We had to pull back, it's too dangerous, he's been there so long his arse has gone numb and his legs are shaking; it could blow any second.'

'So you just left him on his own?' said Danny, angrily pushing past him. 'I'm going in.'

'I've got a duty of care to my men,' the team leader shouted after him.

Danny ignored him and slid inside the warehouse.

CHAPTER 52

The Minister for Defence, David Tremain, sat next to the Prime Minister at the top of a long walnut-veneered conference table in the Cabinet Office Briefing Rooms, more commonly shortened to COBR. The rooms were known as the place for government COBR meetings, triggered by instances of regional or national crises. London's Police Commissioner, the head of the Special Crime and Counter Terrorism Division, and various other members of the cabinet sat down on either side. The room was in a heated discussion about Nicholas Snipe and the missing nuclear device, primarily the lack of progress in his capture and the recovery of the case.

When the phone rang in the middle of the table, the conversation stopped as all eyes centred on the phone. The Prime Minister answered, listening for a few moments before saying, 'Put them through,' before replacing the receiver. 'Gentlemen, there's been a development,' he continued, gesturing towards the wall of screens bursting into life at the end of the room.

Simon and Edward appeared live from the incident room.

'Prime Minister, Ministers, gentlemen, I apologise for the intrusion but we have a development. Twenty minutes ago we received a communication from Nicholas Snipe. In a thirty-second call, he gave us the location of Lieutenant Thomas and Sergeant Burns. It's an empty warehouse in Wandsworth and we have agents in situ. I'm afraid Lieutenant Thomas is dead. But thankfully, Sergeant Burns is still alive, albeit stuck on a chair with an explosive device attached to the underneath. The bomb squad is on the way and we are confident we can get him out safely.'

'Thank you, Simon. Although we are glad that Sergeant Burns will soon be safe, the fact is, we still have a live nuclear device in the hands of a lunatic somewhere in London. Are there any other developments that bring us any closer to finding Mr Snipe or the nuclear device?'

'Due to the nature of the attack at the safe house, we are certain that Nicholas Snipe is working with a four-man Iranian team. One would assume he's negotiated some sort of deal with them, services for the return of the case, that sort of thing. We've tracked two vehicles—a black BMW X5 and a grey Peugeot 5008 from this morning's sighting of Mr Snipe in Notting Hill Gate—across London to the safe house where they abducted Thomas and Burns. In the last few minutes, we've had hits on both vehicles from traffic cameras in Wandsworth, and we're putting cars on all the main routes out of the area,' Edward said.

'Anything on the mobile that was used to call you?'

'He made the call from the Wandsworth area, but the phone went dead immediately after the call,' Simon said.

'Thank you, Simon, Edward. Let us know the second you get anything,' David said, waiting for the screen to go black before continuing. 'Gentlemen, I know it's frustrating.

But the fact is, we are dealing with highly trained individuals, and operating off grid is one of their prime skill sets.'

'So what do you suggest? We do nothing?' the Prime Minister said, annoyed at the lack of progress.

'That's not what I'm saying at all. Simon and Mr Jenkins are doing a sterling job. We've got every available man crunching data, scrolling through hours of camera feeds and, with the help of the Police Commissioner here, half the Met are scouring the streets for them. It's only a matter of time before we find them.'

'Ok, but time is running out. We can keep a lid on the media for the time being, but with all this activity in the capital, they know something's going on. The longer this goes on, the more chance of a leak getting out. If that happens, gentlemen, we'll have widespread panic on our hands,' the Prime Minister said, ending the meeting and rising from his seat.

David finished shaking everyone's hand and headed out with the Police Commissioner beside him.

'Can I drop you anywhere, Jerry?' David said while messaging his driver to meet him out the front of the building.

'No, thank you, I think I'll walk. I could do with some fresh air after that.'

'Yes, I'm sure. I'll let you know of any developments,' said David, spotting his Mercedes S-Class saloon approaching behind a black BMW X5, his driver, Frank, hidden from view by the dark privacy glass. It pulled up alongside, stopping at exactly the right spot for David to open the rear door. As he got in, he noted the BMW in front had stopped thirty metres up the road. It was the same colour and model as the one they were looking for but had a different number plate.

'Frank, have you noticed that BMW at any other point

today?' he said, pulling the door shut before looking forward.

'Relax, Minister, the BMW is with us. Just sit back. We are going for a little drive. Your phone please,' Darius said, swinging around in the front passenger seat to point a gun at him.

David didn't show any emotion. He calmly handed his phone over and sat back while maintaining eye contact with Darius at all times.

'Where's my driver?' he demanded, as the doors clicked locked and the car moved off, the BMW tucking in behind them as they headed towards Trafalgar Square.

'Don't worry, he's safe. My colleagues in the other car are looking after him,' Darius said, nodding towards the BMW.

'Where are you taking me?'

'An old friend of yours would like a word with you, Mr Tremain, or should I call you Howard? No more questions and don't do anything stupid. I'm instructed to get you there alive, not necessarily uninjured.'

David sat very still in the back, outwardly looking calm while inwardly his mind raced over a multitude of scenarios involving trying to unlock the car door to throw himself out, or diving forward to tackle Darius and the driver. None of these played out favourably, so he resigned to waiting until they had reached their destination.

CHAPTER 53

Entering the warehouse, Danny could see Burns shaking on the chair next to the charred remains of Lieutenant Thomas in a square of light on the other side of the empty space. Danny walked towards him, noticing the look of recognition on Sergeant Burns' face as he got closer.

'Alright, Sarge, how are you holding up?' Danny said, trying to look as relaxed as possible.

'I've had better days,' he said, trying to force a smile.

'Just sit tight, Sarge, the bomb squad will be here any minute, mate. They'll soon have you out of here,' Danny said, kneeling down with his head near the floor to look at the device attached to the bottom of the seat. 'So what did Nicholas Snipe have to say for himself?'

'The mad bastard set fire to Thomas and left. He said he had something to do and that he'd be back later.'

'Is that right? Did he have anyone with him?' Danny said, cursing his grumbling shoulder as he lay on the floor to get a better look under the chair.

'Yeah, four of them, Middle Eastern. Spoke Farsi, I picked up a few words in Afghanistan.'

'They're the Iranian Secret Service. I think Snipe's done some sort of deal with them. He has something they want,' Danny said, rubbing his finger along the lump of plastic explosive before putting it to his nose to sniff it. He frowned and followed the wiring to a battery compartment, then onto a black tube stuck to the underside of the seat. Sliding out, Danny sat upright and got to his feet, awkwardly trying to avoid twisting and pushing up as they aggravated his injuries.

'Where's the bloody bomb squad?' Burns said.

'Just keep calm, Sarge. You know, a cynical man might wonder why Snipe didn't just kill you. He went to all the trouble of kidnapping you, and then leaves you sitting here.'

'Thanks a bunch. Who knows, the man's insane.'

'Perhaps he's not as mad as we think he is,' Danny said, turning his head at the sound of the warehouse doors opening.

Two men shuffled in wearing anti-blast armoured suits and visored helmets,

'Hello, here comes the cavalry. Right, I'm going to leave you in the bomb squad's capable hands.'

'Danny.'

'Yes Sarge,' Danny said, turning back to look at him.

'Thanks for waiting with me. You didn't have to.'

'Yeah, I did,' Danny said with a wry smile, before giving the men in blast suits a nod and walking out.

He headed across to the car, squinting until his eyes got accustomed to the bright sunshine.

'Is the sergeant alright?' Tom asked.

'He'll be fine. The bomb looks fairly basic. I don't think it'll take them long to disarm it.'

'At least with the doctor and the sergeant that's two we've managed to save from Snipe.'

'I don't think Snipe had any intention of killing the sergeant. I think he's playing with us, the booby-trapped seat, the phone call. He wanted us all here,' Danny said to Tom as the bomb squad gave the all clear and the paramedic headed in to take care of Burns.

'So what the hell is he up to?' Tom said, thinking out loud.

'I don't know, but whatever it is, I've got a really bad feeling about it. Come on, let's get back to HQ.'

CHAPTER 54

Just outside London, Snipe pulled up to the rusty gates outside of the old Project Jericho research centre. It hadn't been touched since he, Danny and the others had left all those years ago. He walked to the boot and fetched a brand new set of bolt croppers he'd picked up from a Toolstation on the way there. After cutting through the chain, he pushed the gates open. Snipe walked to the guard hut and smashed the glass in the door with the bolt croppers, running them around the frame to clear any sharp fragments out of the way before climbing through. When he reached a small metal lockbox mounted on the wall, he pulled his gun, stood back, and shot the small stainless steel lock out. The door swung open, displaying all the keys to the facility, hung on little hooks organised by numbered and coloured key rings in typical military fashion.

Snipe looked around, his eyes falling on a wastepaper bin. He picked it up, unhooking and throwing the keys into the bin before hitting the button to raise the barrier on his way out. He drove into the car park, not caring where he left the car. It wasn't like anyone would see it.

'Are you coming or are you just going to sit there and sulk?' Snipe said, getting out of the car to head for the entrance door, his hand fishing through the keys in the bin until he found the right one.

'I still say you should have fried that sergeant like the other one.'

Snipe turned back from the open door and watched his brother's image melt out through the car door before following him inside.

'It's like chess, Tel, you sacrifice the pawns to check-mate the king. Come on, we've got work to do,' Snipe said with a big grin.

'Chess! Since when did you play fucking chess?' Terry answered back grumpily.

'Since these fuckers messed with my head, that's when,' Snipe growled back.

He wandered around the research centre, looking in the labs and treatment rooms that triggered memories like waves rolling through his head.

'Hey bruv, time's getting on, you've got to get things ready for them.'

Snipe looked over and nodded to his brother. He went back to the car and grabbed a sports bag before heading across to the accommodation block and the gymnasium.

'You know Darius and his men are going to kill you the second you give them that case, don't you?' Terry said.

'The thought had crossed my mind,' Snipe chuckled.

'So you've got a plan?'

'What the hell are you asking me for, dickhead, you're in my head, not real, a figment of my imagination. You know what I'm fucking thinking,' Snipe shouted, the image of Terry suddenly vanishing, leaving him feeling strangely alone. 'Tel, Terry, bruv.'

He turned three hundred and sixty degrees before standing still.

'He's gone,' Snipe muttered to himself.

'You ever talk to me like that again, and I'll knock you into the middle of next week.'

He turned to see Terry sitting on a weights bench, staring angrily back at him. Snipe's mouth curled up into a grin, and his eyes widened before he laughed uncontrollably.

'I'm glad you find me so fucking amusing, you wanker,' Terry added, the comment only making Snipe laugh harder.

He eventually got control of himself before checking his watch.

'Come on, they'll be here in the morning. Let's check out my old room,' he said, grabbing the sports bag.

CHAPTER 55

The next morning, the incident room continued to be a hive of tense activity, with dozens of agents analysing hundreds of streams of information in the hope of a breakthrough. Danny paced around the information screens, frustrated at Snipe's ability to keep one step ahead of them, while Simon and Edward continually moved new information around the touch screens with patient professionalism.

After opening and expanding a flagged file, Edward shouted over the drone of voices in the room. 'Listen up. I need someone to go out to Cowley Mill Trading Estate in Uxbridge. We have a traffic camera that picked up a Peugeot 5008 late yesterday afternoon. It matches our target vehicle but has false plates that don't match the vehicle type.'

'I'll go. I can't sit around here any longer. It's driving me mad,' Danny said.

'Are you sure? It's probably nothing,' said Edward, happy to send someone else.

'It's ok, I could do with the drive. What have you got?'

'Like I said, we have a traffic camera at the entrance to the estate,' Edward said, pulling up a picture of a Peugeot 5008 entering the industrial estate on the monitor and another showing the rear of the vehicle as it left twenty minutes later. The sun was on the windscreen, making it impossible to see the driver, but the car matched the one they were looking for. 'The registration number belongs to a Jaguar F-Pace from Lewisham. It could be a mistake, or a tax dodger or a stolen car. It seems unlikely it's one of our suspects. There are no empty units and no businesses there that are in the police or our systems with criminal links. I just need someone to go there and show Snipe's picture around to eliminate it.'

'Yeah, I can do that,' Danny said, glad to get out.

'Do you want me to come with you?' Tom said, poking his head up from behind a computer terminal.

'Nah, you're alright, mate. To be honest, I could do with some thinking time.'

'Ok,' Tom said, understanding what he meant.

Once again, Danny headed down to the underground car park and jumped into his car parked next to Simon's Range Rover. This time he reversed out of the parking place and drove out onto London's streets at a more sedate pace, crawling through traffic until he joined the A40 to pick up speed as he headed out of the capital.

CHAPTER 56

Snipe watched the BMW X5 and David Tremain's Mercedes S-Class saloon approaching through the woods from a first-floor window.

'Time for kick off, Tel.'

'Yeah, how about you try not to fuck it up, for once in your life,' Terry's voice echoed in his head.

'That's funny, bruv, because I ain't the one who got themselves killed, am I?' Snipe bit back, peeling himself away from the window to head down the stairs.

'Bring him in here,' Snipe shouted across to Darius when they were parked.

Snipe watched them march David Tremain and another man into the building at gunpoint, their hands tied behind their backs and a strip of gaffer tape wound across their mouths and around their heads. They followed Snipe into the sports hall.

'Who the fuck's that?' Snipe said, looking at the second man.

'It's his driver,' said Darius when they were inside.

'It's not two-for-one week. What the fuck do I need a

230

driver for?' Snipe growled, his gun out and aimed before anyone could move, the gunshot echoing around the hall as he shot the driver in the head.

Four guns flew up in Snipe's direction as Darius's men stood either side of David Tremain, itching to pull the triggers.

'We brought you what you wanted. Now, where's the case?' Darius said, without lowering his gun.

'Whoa, Darius, and there's me thinking we were buddies. My brother warned me about you. You stick him down over there first,' Snipe said, moving over to a weights bench, clicking the back up so David had to sit upright on it.

When he was down, Snipe picked at the end of the gaffer tape and ripped it off his mouth.

'You'll pay for killing my driver. I promise you, I'll have them track you down and have you terminated,' David said, his voice calm and no sign of fear showing in his face.

'Fuck me, everyone's a right bundle of fun today. Just put a cork in it and sit tight, David. David! What kinda fucking name is David? Did you make that up? Because I liked you better when you were Howard,' Snipe said, fixing David's hands behind the seat with heavy duty zip ties.

'The case,' Darius demanded, his hand tensing around the handgun by his side.

'Alright, take it easy, Darius. I've got your case.'

'Where is it?'

Snipe fixed him with a stare, his grin dropping as his face went serious.

'You know, a cynical man might think you'll put a bullet in my head the second I give you the case,' he said calmly.

'We have a deal,' Darius said, holding Snipe's stare.

'I'll tell you what, you and Ball-bag stay here and look

after our guest, and I'll take Kevlar and Fajita with me to get the case.'

While Darius decided the best response, Babak, Kaveh, and Farid looked at Snipe, itching to kill him for taking the piss out of their names.

'Kaveh, Farid, go with him and get the case,' Darius eventually said.

'Great, peachy, this way, chaps, follow me,' said Snipe, his face breaking back into a grin as he moved to the door and waved them after him.

Kaveh and Farid followed him out the door, heading off down the corridor before disappearing out of sight.

'You know he's going to kill you all,' said David calmly.

'Shut up,' Darius shouted, turning to punch David in the stomach, leaving him coughing and retching.

Snipe pushed the entrance doors open and led Farid and Kaveh across the path to the research building next door.

'Come on, guys, why look so glum? You're getting your case back. You can fuck off back to the land of dry dirt and camel shit. You should be happy,' Snipe said, chuckling as he opened the research building entrance doors. 'It's just down here.'

They followed him down a clinical-looking corridor all the way to the end where he turned right and opened the door to the nearest room. They followed him into the x-ray machine waiting room, where Snipe gestured through the open metal door to the dark room beyond.

'It's in there on the x-ray bed, here let me put the light on for you,' Snipe said, turning for the switch on the wall as Farid and Kaveh took a step inside.

The harsh strip lights burst into life, leaving them blinking at an empty x-ray bed. As they turned, the heavy metal door slammed shut. The two men gripped the handle and pounded on its surface, but the door wouldn't budge. Snipe's grinning face came into view through the thick glass viewing window. He pressed the button on the microphone, and the speakers clicked inside.

'Hey guys, my brother thinks you don't look too good. He thinks we should take a quick x-ray.'

'I'm going to kill you,' Farid yelled, taking his gun out and firing into the thick glass. It chipped and pitted, but the bullets didn't get through the protective laminate layer put there to stop the x-ray radiation.

'That's a bit rude, Tel. Shall we?'

'Yeah, fucking fry the bastards, bruv.'

Snipe flicked a couple of switches and grabbed the joystick, then leaned to one side to see the two robotic arms behind Farid rise up and the heads swivel forwards.

'Move out of the way, you silly bastard, I can't see,' Snipe grumbled, placing his hand on the power dial before cranking it to max.

Snipe could hear a low hum coming from inside the room and leaned in to get a better look at Kaveh and Farid. Nothing seemed to be happening. They both stepped back and aimed their guns at the glass, firing in unison. It chipped, and cracks creeped across the surface but it didn't give way.

'What's wrong with this piece of shit? I thought you took the power safety module out,' Terry said, leaning in beside Snipe to stick his finger up at Kaveh and Farid.

'I did. Ah, this is no fun, I'll just have to go in there and finish them off myself,' Snipe said, standing up out of the chair.

'Hang on, bruv.'

As he looked to the side of the glass, through a section free of chips and cracks, he could see Kaveh drop his gun and put his hands to his head. A second later, Farid did the same. Kaveh dropped to his knees, screaming as blood started to stream from his tear ducts, nose, and ears.

'Now, this is more like it. Do you think his head will explode, like that film we used to like as kids?' Snipe said, glancing across to Terry.

'What, Scanners?'

'Yeah, Scanners, I bloody loved that film.'

As Kaveh fell on his front, Farid staggered forward, slapping his hands and head onto the glass surface, spitting blood out as he said something in his native tongue before sliding down to the floor below.

Ignoring the red flashing lights and the alarm that started sounding, Snipe stood on tiptoe so he could look down at them, his eyes fixated as he watched them curl up into a fetal position and die. The console sparked and went up in a puff of smoke before the x-ray room went silent, the robotic arms sinking slowly down to their standby position.

'Bummer, their heads didn't explode. Right, let's take care of Darius and Ball-bag,' Snipe muttered, instantly bored with the deaths of Kaveh and Farid.

CHAPTER 57

'Y ou've still got time, you know,' David said once he'd gotten his breath back.

'Time for what, Englishman?' Babak grunted.

Darius just glanced at him dismissively before turning his head back to the entrance doors to the sports hall.

'When Snipe comes back, kill him and turn the case over to me. I give you my word as Minister for Defence. I'll send you back to Iran with full diplomatic immunity. The case's existence and your country's involvement in creating it will be kept a secret. No political escalation, no need to involve the U.S. about the breach in sanctions on your nuclear weapons capability. Everybody's happy,' David said, his voice calm, his reasoning making Babak look to Darius for comment.

'He opens his mouth again, you put a bullet in his head. We stick to the plan,' Darius growled back, his eyes leaving the entrance doors to give David a look to say he meant it.

'Hi honey, we're home,' came Snipe's voice from somewhere down the corridor.

As Darius and Babak turned to look, Snipe's arm whipped around the door as he threw a stun grenade into the hall. With lightning reflexes, Darius dived through the serving hatch into the kitchen, sending utensils and metal serving trays crashing around him. He hit the kitchen floor awkwardly, losing his gun, which rattled off under the gas hobs. The grenade went off a split second later, its flash whiting out Babak's vision while the ear-shattering explosion temporarily deafened him to all but a high-pitched whistle. He never saw Snipe enter the hall with a gun in each hand. He tapped each trigger, sending two bullets into Babak's heart and blowing him off his feet, dead before he hit the floor.

'Sit tight, Minister, I'll get to you in a bit,' Snipe said to David before sprinting towards the kitchen, firing through the hatch to keep Darius's head down as he picked up pace. Changing his aim at the last minute, Snipe emptied the clip of one gun into the lock of the kitchen door that sat to one side of the serving hatch. The lock disintegrated as Snipe dropped the empty gun and shoulder charged its wooden surface. He burst through the kitchen in a shower of flying bits of wood and metal, the entrance taking Darius by surprise.

Seeing Snipe move his other gun towards him, Darius heaved a stainless-steel preparation table up on end in front of him. Little round dents popped inwards inches from his face as he tucked in behind it. Adrenaline pumping through his veins, Darius grabbed each side of the table, yelling as he picked it up, and charged at Snipe with the table in front of him like a shield. He could feel jolts up his arms as Snipe emptied his gun into the table's surface, more little round dents drawing a line down the table's centre just before he smacked into Snipe, smashing him backwards into a tall refrigerator.

The advantage only lasted a split second. Snipe grabbed the side of the table and ripped it out of his grip, throwing it to one side, where it jammed into the doorway. Snipe charged at Darius, his eyes wide and excited, grinning as he buzzed on the adrenaline of battle.

Darius remained level-headed, his training and muscle memory kicking in to block and counter Snipe's punches, elbows and kicks. The fight moved to the back of the kitchen, where Darius grabbed a heavy pan off the side and cracked it into the side of Snipe's head. The blow knocked Snipe's head to one side. He stepped back, straightened his head up, and touched the trickle of blood running down his temple with his fingers. As he looked at the blood on his fingers, his face contorted with insane rage. He sprung forward at Darius, swiping the pan to one side when he swung it back at him.

The blows came fast and furious. Darius tried to block and counter, but Snipe seemed oblivious to them as his rage grew and grew. As Darius weakened, Snipe grabbed his jacket and flattened him onto the stainless-steel worktop, sliding him through the pots and pans towards the row of knives lined up on a magnetic strip fixed to the wall. Pinning him down with a hand on his throat, Snipe grabbed a carving knife off the strip and thrust it down towards Darius's heart. Both hands shot up to grab Snipe's wrist just as the tip of the blade touched the material of his jacket. Darius looked up at Snipe with a steely determination. Pushing with all his might, he inched the blade away. Snipe released the grip on Darius's throat and pounded his palm on top of the knife handle to push down with two hands and all his body weight. The tip of the blade jerked back down, pushing into the material until it tore through and sliced into the top layer of flesh.

Darius pushed the knife back, shaking with the exertion. They stayed there motionless, locked in a muscular stalemate, until Snipe's strength and bodyweight overpowered Darius's screaming muscles. His eyes turned from steely determination to the fear of the inevitable. As Snipe stared and grinned down at him, the blade slid a millimetre at a time into Darius's chest.

'No, argh, I—'

Darius's plea just excited Snipe all the more. As the knife split his heart in two, he coughed up blood. His body shuddered, then fell still. Darius's eyes looked into Snipe's for a few seconds before looking up at the ceiling lifelessly.

Snipe let go of the knife and stood staring at Darius for a minute or two. Eventually, his breathing went back to normal, and his body relaxed. He walked away, pulling the table from the doorway before walking casually back towards David.

'Right, where were we?' Snipe said, his grin returning.

He moved to the sports bag and pulled out a laptop and turned it on. It took a minute or two to boot up and for the 4G mobile dongle to lock onto a signal. When it was ready, Snipe opened up multiple live webcam views of the Thames, central London and the SIS building.

'You want to know a little secret, Minister? Your pal Simon did me a favour and drove the Iranian nuke right underneath the SIS building. Hey, don't look so sad. I brought you here to watch, so you didn't feel left out,' Snipe said, placing the laptop on the weights bench next to David.

David refrained from commenting. There was nothing he could say to this madman that would do any good.

'Right, what's next? Oh yeah, time to invite our special guest.'

CHAPTER 58

Grateful to be away from the pressure cooker environment of the incident room, Danny stopped to get a coffee on the way through Uxbridge before driving to the industrial estate. He parked up, looking at the assortment of small and large works units on either side of him as he sipped his drink. It looked like a waste of time, but as he was here, he finished his coffee and took a walk around the units.

Flashing his MI6 ID badge as he entered, he asked if anyone had seen the picture of Snipe he had on his phone from a CCTV still taken at Notting Hill Gate. After asking at a tyre centre, garages, and a tile and bathroom show-room with no result, he'd had enough. He headed back towards the car along the last strip of units, stopping to let a workman pass as he came out of a Toolstation store carrying a bundle of three-metre-long electrical trunking in his arms. Danny glanced at the open door and thought, what the hell, he'd try one more. Approaching the counter, he flashed his badge to the man serving. The green-haired guy with way too much metal poking out from the many piercings in his face looked blankly back at him.

'Excuse me, sir, have you or any of your colleagues seen this man in here?' Danny said half-heartedly, ready for a 'no, sorry' answer, so he could get on his way back to London.

'Yeah, he was in here. He was, like, a really weird guy, mad eyes. He bought some bolt croppers and cable ties then left. The dude was, like, talking to himself.'

'What, really? You're sure?' Danny said, surprised.

'Positive, man. If you'd seen him, you'd remember him too. Something real unnerving about the guy.'

'Thanks, that's great,' Danny said, calling Edward as he left the building.

'Ed, it's Danny, the Peugeot in Uxbridge, it was Snipe. He bought bolt cutters and zip ties from a Toolstation outlet.'

Danny paused while he listened to Edward address the incident room.

'Everyone quiet. Nicholas Snipe was at an industrial estate in Uxbridge at three thirty yesterday afternoon. I want all units out to Uxbridge now. He bought bolt cutters and zip ties, so I want every empty building, gated compound—anywhere where bolt cutters would gain you entry—checked, and checked now.'

Danny could hear the room behind Edward explode into a hum of activity before Edward came back on the phone.

'Good work. We'll take over from here. Get yourself back to HQ.'

'Ok, I'll see you in a bit,' Danny said, hanging up and heading back to the car. He'd only gone a few feet before the phone rang in his hand. Danny looked at the no caller

ID displayed on the screen and held it to his ear without speaking.

'Ooh, the silent treatment, you're sending chills down my spine,' Snipe chuckled.

'What do you want, Snipe?' Danny replied bluntly.

'I've organised a little reunion party for us. It's going to be great. I've even got beer and nibbles in. Here, say hello to one of the guests.'

Danny listened as the phone went quiet. He could hear some sort of background noise before a slapping sound and somebody grunting.

'Don't do anything he says, Daniel, he's—' Another slapping sound cut David Tremain's voice short, followed by a grunt as Snipe knocked the wind out of him.

'Sorry, mate, I think our Minister for Defence has had a little too much to drink. He never could hold his liquor. Anyway, jump in your motor and head out of London to meet us.'

'Where are you?' Danny said, already running to the car with a pretty good idea where Snipe was anyway.

'The old Project Jericho building, where it all began. Come alone, matey boy. If I see anyone other than you coming down that drive, I send one message and a few million Londoners get an all-over tan. Hurry up, pal, clock's ticking.'

'I'm at the SIS building. It'll take a while to get there,' Danny said, trying to buy himself some time.

'Well, stop talking to me and drive then,' Snipe chuckled, hanging up.

Danny sat with the engine running, staring at his phone, decisions and scenarios running through his head. He couldn't risk calling it in. Snipe would kill David and detonate the nuke the minute a strike team moved in. He had to go himself and use the element of surprise. Snipe thought he was driving from central London, not from half an hour down the road.

Fuck it.

Putting the car in gear, Danny wheelspun out of the estate and headed towards the Project Jericho research building.

CHAPTER 59

Taking the narrow country lanes way too fast, Danny overshot the turning in the woods for Project Jericho's research buildings. He locked the wheels up and slid to a stop before jamming the car in reverse and hurtling backwards so he could turn down the long drive. With the sun going down and dense forest on either side of the drive, the dark grey strip of tarmac was barely visible as it headed off through the trees. Not daring to put the headlights on and announce his arrival, Danny drove slowly, pulling the car to a stop when the floodlights from the research centre in the distance cut beams of light around the tree trunks between him and the perimeter fence. Taking his Glock 17 handgun from its shoulder holster, Danny turned the internal door light off before opening the car door. He stepped out into the dark, stretched, and rolled his injured shoulder, before twisting at the waist, cursing the grumbling pain from both healing bullet wounds.

'Suck it up, Danny boy. You need all your wits about you to deal with this bastard,' he muttered to himself, checking the time by the luminous paint on the face of his G-Shock watch.

Good, he won't be expecting me for another forty-five minutes. Time for a recce.

Moving in the darkness of the tree line, Danny headed towards the main gate. He crouched down behind the branches of the last line of trees, looking across the cleared patch of ground before the security fence that ran around the facility. The place was all lit up, but looked old and unused for years. Moss grew on the security hut roof by the open gated entrance, and the grass around the two research buildings was knee high. Three cars sat in the car park: the BMW X5, Peugeot 5008, and David Tremain's Mercedes S-Class saloon.

Jesus, three cars. The Iranians must be here with him.

Danny's heart sank. He'd been so engrossed with the thought of getting Snipe that he'd forgotten about the Iranians. One-on-one in his present state was bad enough, but one-on-five was suicide.

He stayed crouched in the shadows, deciding whether to call for help or go in and use the only advantage he had, the element of surprise.

'For fuck's sake, why does this always happen to me?' Danny muttered.

He shook his head and took three deep breaths, exploding out of the tree line as he sprinted across open ground as fast as he could. As he moved through the gate, he spun and flattened his back against the security hut. Breathing heavily against the brickwork, Danny looked around the hut at the two buildings across the car park. They still looked quiet, old and abandoned, like a film set from some dystopian deserter movie. After taking a few more deep breaths, Danny ran fast and low to the back of the BMW X5, bobbing down behind it out of sight. He checked his watch.

I'm still ahead. I've got to get moving.

He checked the two buildings one last time for movement, then ran for the research building, flattening himself against the brickwork when he got there. Ducking down, Danny moved under the windows until he reached the entrance doors. Darting his head forward, he peered through the glass at the deserted corridor inside. The lights were all on, and when he tried the door, it was unlocked. Opening it slowly, he slid inside, keeping his hand on the door handle to take the tension off of the closer until it shut silently.

He stood inside, motionless, slowing his breathing as he listened for telltale signs of movement. When none presented themselves, he moved down the corridor, listening to the other side of doors before entering each room, his gun up and ready for Snipe or the Iranians.

The place was quiet and empty. When he got to the end of the corridor, he could smell acrid, burning plastic in the air. A faint smokey haze floated below the strip lights in the ceiling. The door to the x-ray room was open, and the smell got stronger as he approached. Looking inside, Danny could see a black scorch mark on the control panel on the desk and the bullet-ridden viewing window above it. He unlocked the metal door, pushing it open until it stuck on an obstacle on the other side. Sliding his head through, Danny saw Farid and Kaveh's bodies curled up on the floor behind it. Dried blood lines out of their eyes, ears, and nose led to a sticky pool of blood on the floor.

Snipe double-crossed them. I can't say I'm surprised. At least I won't have the Iranians to deal with as well as him.

Squeezing through, Danny bobbed down and felt for a

pulse on both bodies to be sure they were dead, before sliding back out into the waiting room and heading back the way he came. He checked his watch again, then ran across the short stretch of open space to the accommodation block.

CHAPTER 60

'Come on, people, we need a breakthrough here. Anything we can use to pin down the location of Nicholas Snipe and the Iranians,' Simon spoke loudly as the room hushed and looked at him.

As soon as he'd finished, the paused room hit play and resumed its thrum of voices on phones, people moving around, and keyboards clicking.

'Has Mr Pearson checked in yet?'

'No sir, I'll call him now,' Tom said, looking up from a computer.

Simon moved his attention back to the main screens and their wealth of information offering up everything he wanted to know about what had happened, but nothing about what was happening now, this instant. He turned back to the room and watched the dozens of men analysing thousands of CCTV camera feeds and processing every sighting of Peugeot 5008's and BMW X5's. The odd sight of a car wheel leaning against the wall at the back of the room caught his attention. He walked over to it, looking at the size and style of the alloy wheel inside the tyre, noting that it looked similar to that of his Range Rover.

'What's this wheel doing here?' he said, addressing the room.

'It's the object from the partial match CCTV footage, sir. I had traffic pick it up and bring it in.'

'What partial match footage, er...?' Simon said, prompting him for a name.

'Trevor, sir. We had a partial match on a piece of CCTV footage from ten past four yesterday morning. The quality was very poor, so I put it through the enhancement program. With the priority on the vehicle searches I haven't had chance to look at it again,' Trevor said, tapping away on the keyboard before bringing it up on one of the main screens. The enhancement had cleaned the image up to see the back of a man around Snipe's shape and size walking down a road carrying the wheel before throwing it into a hedge. He turned his head slightly as he did so to reveal a side profile that Simon instantly recognised.

'What make and model of car does that wheel belong to?' Simon said with an urgency to his voice.

'It's from a Range Rover SV, 2020 to present day,' Trevor said, looking up from his notes.

'Where?'

'Er, from camera 2664.'

'No, the location. Where was it taken? Where exactly is camera 2664?' Simon ordered.

Trevor tapped away on his keyboard again, bringing in a map of the whole of London before it zoomed in on a road in St John's Wood Road and the camera location seventy metres from Simon's house.

'Tom, come with me. Now!' Simon yelled over the room, leaving a puzzled Trevor to head for the door.

'Coming, boss,' Tom said, hanging up on his third unanswered call to Danny.

'What's going on?' Tom said when he caught up with Simon in the lift.

'I think Snipe's put something in my car.'

'An explosive device?'

'Maybe, maybe something else. All I know is my spare tyre is sitting in the room upstairs after Snipe took it out of my car at four o'clock yesterday morning. You were the regiment's explosives expert before you joined us. I just need you to take a quick look before I call in the bomb squad.'

'Yes sir,' Tom said as the lift doors slid open in the underground car park.

Simon pulled the key out of his pocket as they approached the Range Rover and was about to unlock it when Tom stopped him.

'Whoa, hang on, sir, let me have a look first.'

Tom moved over to the car and bobbed down. He took his phone out and turned the torch light on, methodically moving it around the crack between the bonnet and the body shell before checking wheel arches, and the crack between the boot and car body. When he'd finished, he lay on his back and slid his head under the car, shining his light as he worked his way from the engine compartment, around the sides, to under the rear of the vehicle.

'Got something, sir. Two wires coming out of the drain plug under the spare tyre compartment, they're spliced into the car's wiring loom,' Tom said, sliding back out and standing up.

'Let's get the bomb squad in.' Simon was quickly reaching for his phone.

'Hang on a minute, sir, you've been in and out of this car all day, right?'

'Right.'

'So whatever it is, it's not rigged to the locking mechanism, the doors, or the ignition. So let's have a look at what we're dealing with,' said Tom, pointing to the nearest concrete support pillar in the underground car park. 'Maybe unlock it from behind that, just in case,' he added with a smile.

Tucked in behind the pillar, Simon pressed the unlock button, relieved to hear the usual pips and click of the door locks unlocking. Moving to the boot, Tom waved his foot under the back, which made the boot open automatically. After taking Simon's coat, umbrella, and usual boot stuff out, Tom pulled a Swiss Army knife from his pocket and unfolded the blade. He carefully lifted the corner of the boot carpet a couple of millimetres, shining the light from his phone underneath as he bobbed down to look into the gap. He did this all the way around until he was satisfied it wasn't booby-trapped, then lifted the cover up, flipping it back to expose a large sports bag sitting in the spare wheel space.

Wiping the sweat off his hands onto his jeans, Tom tentatively unzipped the bag one tooth at a time, peeling the nylon material aside to expose the Iranian scientist's nuclear device. Snipe had disabled the key section to arm and disarm the device, with two cables soldered to its circuit board before leading out the bottom of the bag and through a drain hole to the underside of the car. The LCD display glowed, lighting up Tom and Simon's faces in a ghoulish green from the word Armed written across it.

'Can you disarm it?' said Simon.

'Probably, given enough time. Better let the experts deal with it. Call the bomb squad in,' Tom said as they both backed away from the boot.

Simon nodded in agreement and made the call. While

he was on the phone, Tom called Edward in the incident room upstairs.

'Tom, where the hell did you and Simon disappear to? I can't get hold of Daniel, and David Tremain's secretary's just contacted us to say he hasn't turned up for any of his appointments today and isn't answering his phone.'

'Sorry, Ed, we've been a little busy. I've got some good news and bad news.'

'Go on, Tom,' Edward said, puzzled.

'The good news is we've found the nuclear bomb.'

'Why is it I don't I think I'm going to like the next bit?'

'The bad news is that it's armed and booby-trapped into the boot of Simon's car. He's on the phone to the bomb squad as we speak.'

'Christ, should we evacuate the building?' Edward said, looking around at all his agents working away.

'No, not much point. It'd only cause panic, and they wouldn't be able to get far enough away. If it detonates, it'll take out most of central London. Look, at the moment it's just armed, not counting down to detonate, so let's just keep calm until the bomb squad get here to deal with it. Hang on, Edward. What did they say, Simon?'

'They're on their way with a police escort. ETA, twenty minutes.'

'They'll be here in twenty minutes, Ed.'

'Ok, I'll get onto security to clear the way for them,' Edward said, hanging up.

They both instinctively looked at their watches, then turned in unison to look at the nuclear device with its LCD display lighting up the boot.

'Did I hear you say David Tremain and Pearson have gone missing?' Simon finally said.

'Yep, this day just gets better and better,' Tom replied, looking at his watch for the third time in a minute.

CHAPTER 61

'C'hin up, David, our special guest star will be here soon. Relax, watch some TV,' Snipe said, pointing to a laptop sat on the weights bench beside David, still displaying live webcam views of the Thames, central London, and the SIS building.

'Bit bloody small, isn't it? I can hardly make the buildings out,' Terry's voice rang out in Snipe's head.

Snipe frowned as he looked at the small screen.

'Mmm, you're right, Tel, that won't do at all. The minister here needs to see it clearly the minute Simon and all the other bastards get it. Burned up in glorious technicolour, fucking high definition, mushroom cloud.'

Snipe turned away from talking to the empty space behind David. He glanced at his watch, then looked at the entrance doors in deep thought. 'I've still got time before he arrives. There's got to be a large monitor or TV around here somewhere,' he said, heading out into the corridor.

On the other side of the building, Danny forced the lock on a fire escape door and entered the building through the laundry room. He moved silently over to the door and put his ear to its surface. All was quiet. Sliding out into the corridor, Danny moved along, listening for any sounds of movement. As he passed the main entrance doors, he heard a metallic clanging. Looking down the sights of his gun, Danny moved towards the noise, stopping every few feet to check behind him before moving on. When he reached the doors of the sports hall, Danny slid his back against the brickwork on one side, darting his head across to get a snapshot of the hall through the glass panel in the door. He processed the image of David straining and throwing himself forward, trying to break the cable ties that bound him to the weights bench. Although he couldn't see the entire hall, the fact that David was trying so hard to free himself told him Snipe wasn't there.

With time and the element of surprise ticking away, Danny went with his gut instinct and pushed through the door. David froze, expecting to see Snipe's insane grin looking back at him, and was relieved to see Danny instead.

'Hang on,' Danny said, seeing David's cable-tied hands.

He ran to the wrecked kitchen, jumped over the bodies of Babak and Darius and grabbed a knife off the magnetic strip on the wall.

'Hurry, he'll be back in a minute,' David said, his eyes glued to the doors of the hall.

'That's it, let's get you out of here,' Danny said, cutting the ties and sliding the knife into his pocket before looking at the laptop and webcam images of central London.

'No, I can't leave. We've got to stop that maniac. The nuclear bomb is in the SIS building. Snipe has planted it in the boot of Simon's car. He's been waiting for you to arrive to activate the timer from his phone.'

Danny stood, thinking, his mind searching for solutions.

He pulled his phone and car keys from his pocket and handed them to David.

'You need to go. My car is down the drive. Get to it, call Simon, then go. I'll try and get the phone off Snipe,' Danny said, his face determined and mind made up.

David knew that look well and reluctantly took the phone and keys with a nod of agreement.

'Right, stay close,' Danny said, moving to the doors with David close behind.

Snipe was busy in the security room over in the far corner of the building. He'd unplugged a large monitor and was about to take it back to the sports hall. Turning around, his eyes fell on the bank of CCTV screens behind him. Movement on the one looking at the main doors caught his eye. He blinked in disbelief as Danny opened the door for David. He could see them exchange a few words before David ran off across the car park. Danny remained inside, pulling the door shut before heading off down the corridor.

'How the fuck did he get here so fast?' Terry growled over his shoulder.

'No, no, no, fucker. There's no way he could have driven from central London that quickly.'

'You've fucked it up again, bruv.'

'Fuck off, you dead bastard!' Snipe shouted, exploding in an uncontrollable rage as he hurled the monitor on the floor. He turned around and punched the CCTV screen repeatedly until it sparked, smoked, and died.

'Bastard, that's it. Forget the show. I'm going to set the timer off now,' he growled, regaining control of his temper. He pulled the burner phone from his pocket, typed a command and hit send. After hearing the beep to confirm the message had been received, Snipe scanned the remaining monitors, spotting Danny moving down a corridor before disappearing out of camera shot.

'Time to finish this,' Snipe muttered, reaching forward to press the talk button on the PA mic sitting on the desk in front of him.

CHAPTER 62

David ran to Danny's car as fast as he could. He slumped into the driver's seat, taking a few deep breaths to calm the adrenaline down enough to stop his hands from shaking as he tried to dial Simon's number.

'Not now, Daniel, this really isn't a good time,' Simon answered before the phone barely had time to ring.

'Wait, Simon, don't hang up, this is David Tremain.'

'David, what? Why are you on Pearson's phone?'

'Doesn't matter, the Iranian nuclear device is in the boot of your car. Snipe's planning to set it off remotely. Do you understand me?' David said as fast as he could.

'It's ok, David, we've already found it. The bomb squad will be here in about ten minutes. Now tell me what's going on.'

'Snipe kidnapped me and took me to the old Project Jericho building. Daniel got me out, he's staying inside to stop Snipe from triggering the bomb.'

'What about the Iranians? Are they still there?' Simon continued while he paced around the car park.

'No, Snipe has killed them all. As soon as the bomb is disarmed, you need to get a team here fast to take Snipe out. I'll stay here. Call me back as soon as it's done.'

'Ok David, I'll get a team on standby. Talk to you soon,' Simon said, hanging up.

Still standing by the boot of Simon's car, Tom turned at the sound of a beep coming from within. As he looked in, the word Armed disappeared from the LCD screen to be replaced by a five-minute clock, which immediately started counting down.

'Er, sir.'

'Just give me a couple of minutes, Tom,' replied Simon without looking at him, his phone already to his ear as he waited to be connected to the task force commander.

'Now, sir, this really won't wait.'

The urgency in Tom's voice made Simon turn, his face falling at the sight of the clock blinking down to four and a half minutes.

'Jesus, the bomb disposal team will never get here in time. Can you stop it?' Simon said, hanging up his call.

'Do I have a choice?' Tom answered, pulling his Swiss Army knife back out, his fingers fumbling as he selected a little pair of wire cutters. 'Could you hold the light up for me, sir?' he continued, passing Simon his phone with the torchlight on. Shaking slightly, both men leaned into the boot.

CHAPTER 63

Danny moved silently along the corridor, checking rooms and listening for any signs of Snipe. The PA speaker above his head whistled into life with loud feedback.

'You and me, Pearson, no guns, a fair fight. You beat me, you get to cancel the timer I've just set running on the nuke. Tick tock, mate, clock's ticking.'

As the announcement faded to silence, Danny heard a door slam somewhere back towards the sports hall. Turning, Danny moved cautiously back the way he came, his eyes and gun sights moving as one as he ignored Snipe's 'no guns, fair fight' comment. The first chance he got, he'd aim at Snipe with a non-lethal shot and force him to disarm the nuke.

He reached the doors to the sports hall, darting his head across as before to get a snapshot of the inside before he attempted to enter. The hall was empty apart from the laptop, which was still playing webcam videos from central London.

Well, at least London's still in one piece.

He'd just placed his hand on the door when the power went out, plunging him into darkness. Danny froze, concentrating on his hearing and sixth sense until his eyes adjusted to the darkness.

There you are.

Footsteps tapped on concrete steps.

He's heading up the stairs.

Moving away from the windowless sports hall, Danny could see the corridor lit up in a dim yellow glow from the lights still on in the car park outside. When he reached the bottom of the stairs, the door to the electrical cupboard beside them was open. Sparks and puffs of smoke flared in the dark from the bashed fuse board inside, a dumbbell from the sports hall lay on the floor below it. Pulling himself away, Danny looked up the centre of the stairwell and darted his head back out of sight as his eyes met with Snipe's looking down at him from the second floor. A low, gravelly chuckle echoed down from above as he moved up the steps. He kept close to the wall, out of sight, placing his feet carefully on each step as he moved silently to the first floor. He whipped in from the first floor landing, his gun pointing straight up in front of him as he targeted the second floor landing.

There was no Snipe, no noise, just shadowy, empty space.

Danny moved up again, pausing just before the second floor landing. He took a quick look, his head shooting into the corridor at floor height. Most people would target the body or head height if they were lying in wait to shoot you. A change of aim takes time and skill, giving you the chance to fold back out of sight. But there was no shot. The dark corridor, dimly lit by the lights outside, was empty.

Danny moved forward, rolling his feet from heel to toe, moving in total silence. He glanced into each bedroom as he went, the metal beds and lockers remaining in the same place they were all those years ago.

At the end of the corridor he reached the door to the toilet block. The hairs on the back of his neck stood up. He could feel Snipe's presence close by. Aiming his gun at the centre of the door, Danny bent his legs ever so slightly, ready to kick the door open and shoot. At that moment, he realised he'd been wrong and started to turn. Snipe burst out of the storage cupboard behind him, his eyes gleaming with crazed excitement and teeth gritted. He whacked the gun out of Danny's hand with a foot-long, solid metal pull-down bar from the multi-gym machine in the sports hall. Snipe followed it by throwing his forehead forward to headbutt Danny between the eyes, knocking him through the door onto the bathroom floor. His gun clattered away across the tiles to the washbasins. Ignoring the pain and blurred vision from his watering eyes, Danny backward rolled into a standing position, his fists raised, ready to fight. But he was a second too late. Snipe planted a boot into his stomach as soon as he was up. The blow sent electric shocks of pain through Danny's core, the healing tissue tearing inside as he flew backwards, snapping the cubicle door off its hinges before cracking his back painfully onto the toilet cistern.

'You're getting soft in your old age, Pearson,' Snipe chuckled.

Seeing Snipe's shadowy outline coming at him fast with the metal bar raised above his head, Danny twisted and grabbed the heavy porcelain cistern lid. He twisted back, swinging it at Snipe with all his might, catching him on the side of the head. The impact sounded like a cricket ball off a bat. Snipe spun off to one side, dropping the metal bar as he disappeared out of sight. Danny pushed himself up off the toilet, trampling on the broken door to get out of the cubicle. Snipe was back on his feet, flicking blood across the cubicle door next to him from his torn ear as he shook his head to clear it.

'Fucking soft, am I?' Danny growled, swinging the cistern lid at Snipe's head for a second go.

Snipe threw his arm up, blocking the blow with the meat of his forearm before lunging forward to punch Danny in his already screaming stomach. He dropped the cistern lid, doubling over as he staggered backwards, still managing to stay upright.

They stood a few metres apart in the semi-darkness, breathing heavily, their eyes locked on each other, watching every tell-tale movement, preparing for an attack or counterattack.

Snipe moved first, a fast lunge forward, his fist heading for Danny's temple from a lightning fast jab. Danny stood upright and twisted, causing Snipe's blow to skim painfully off his injured shoulder. The movement gave Danny the opportunity to power a punch into Snipe's kidneys.

Snipe grunted hard, staggering back towards the open door to the toilet block. Jumping up, Danny planted both feet into Snipe's stomach in a powerful flying kick. Snipe's feet left the floor as he flew back out of the bathroom door, crashing into the storage cupboard opposite. Danny fell back off the kick, landing flat on his back. He rolled over and pushed himself up onto his feet. He'd only taken his eyes off Snipe for a second, but when he looked toward the doorway, he was gone.

The sound of footsteps on stairs echoed back down the corridor. Danny exhaled, his body shaking as he did so. He put a hand on the wall to steady himself, holding his side with the other. The two recovering bullet wounds sent debilitating waves of pain through his body. He took a few deep breaths and gritted his teeth as he looked for his dropped gun with no success. Stumbling out into the corridor, Danny's head turned at the sound of the roof access door clicking shut at the top of the stairs. Every part of his body was saying, 'fuck it, just leave', but the chance he could stop Snipe wiping out central London kept spurring him on. Putting his hand on the bannister, Danny pulled himself up a step at a time towards the door to the roof.

Here we go again. I'm too old for this shit.

Danny pushed the door slowly open. A floodlight on the brickwork above him lit the flat roof up with its air conditioning units, pipes, and vents. Snipe stood on the far side, pointing a gun straight at him.

'Put it down, Snipe, you didn't do all this just to shoot me. Let's finish this man to man. You win, you kill me. I win, I get the phone to stop the nuke.'

Snipe's mouth curled up into a grin. He placed the gun on top of an air conditioning unit before pulling the phone out of his pocket.

'Just text stop, if you can. You better hurry though, time's nearly up,' Snipe said, shaking the phone before placing it next to the gun.

His grin dropped, and his face hardened as he looked murderously at Danny.

Danny's eyes narrowed, the muscles in his cheeks flexing as he gritted his teeth. Both men bent their knees ever so slightly, tensing their muscles, never taking their eyes off each other. They stayed that way for several seconds, until, as if by some unseen command, they both exploded into action, sprinting towards each other as fast as they could go.

CHAPTER 64

'T om!' Simon was getting agitated.

'Yeah, I know,' Tom said, wiping the sweat out of his eyes as the timer clicked down to two minutes.

He leaned back into the boot, laying his head on the floor, as he tried to trace a loom of blue, red and green wires from the timer unit circuit board as they disappeared under the metal cylinders containing the radioactive material.

'Can't you isolate the detonator or disconnect the timer?' Simon questioned, poking his head into the boot.

'That's not helping, sir, this isn't some crude roadside IED. I don't even know what half the stuff in here does,' Tom replied impatiently.

'Sorry,' Simon said apologetically, moving back out of the way to give Tom some space to work.

'That one is the power to the timer. That one is the anti-tamper circuit to stop you from shutting the timer down. So, these three must be positive, negative, and ground, or is it positive, negative, and tamper circuit?' Tom guessed, thinking out loud, his fingers following a green, red and black loom of wires as they ran from the timer circuit board before disappearing under a metal box fixed between the two large cylinders.

'One minute, thirty, Tom,' Simon announced from behind him.

'Ok, ok. If I can just see under this box,' Tom said, trying to lever it up far enough to see underneath it.

The box wouldn't budge, so he folded the Phillips head screwdriver out of his Swiss Army knife and started unscrewing the box unit off the metal framework that held the components of the bomb together. He loosened it enough to see the black wire grounded to the frame, leaving the green and red going underneath to what he recognised as the detonator.

'Tom, fifty seconds. If you're going to do something, now is the time,' Simon said, speaking quickly.

Tom didn't reply. He finished unscrewing the box off the frame, moving it gently to one side to give himself a clear view of the detonator. To his dismay, the green and red wires hooked around the side of the detonator to terminals on the underside.

'Twenty seconds, Tom,' said Simon, the panic showing in his voice.

'I don't know which one. It's the green or red, but I can't see under the detonator.'

'Ten seconds, Tom.'

'Green, I'm going green.'

With shaking hands, Tom slid the little wire cutters around the green wire, squeezing slowly until the blades cut into the soft plastic sheath.

'Five seconds.'

Tom stopped. 'No, it's red,' he blurted out, sliding the

cutters off the green and onto the red wire to snip it as the timer hit two seconds.

Both Tom and Simon tensed and shut their eyes. They remained that way for a few seconds before opening one eye, then the other, to see that the timer on the bomb had counted down to zero without detonating.

'Oh, thank god,' Tom finally said, taking a deep breath and standing up out of the boot on shaky legs.

'Good work, Tom. Too close for comfort, but good work.' Relief showed on Simon's face as he patted Tom on the back. A second later, his face fell as he remembered David's call before the timer started counting down.

'Shit, I've got to get a team to the Project Jericho building. Tom, you call David Tremain. He's on Daniel's phone. Tell him the bomb is disarmed and tell him to sit tight. A team is on their way.'

'On it,' Tom said, immediately calling Danny's number while Simon got on the phone to the commander of a team that technically didn't exist.

CHAPTER 65

Danny and Snipe covered the distance to the centre of the roof in no time. Danny's plan from the off was to ignore the idea of retribution by a fair fight to the death. Instead, he planned to sidestep Snipe and head straight for the phone and gun, sending the message to stop the bomb a second before putting a bullet in Snipe's head. The plan didn't work. As Danny ducked to the right, Snipe twisted with lightning reflexes. A fist shot out to land heavily on the side of Danny's head. It sent him spiralling off balance to fly backwards over a long section of metal ventilation ducting. He landed heavily on his injured shoulder and grunted out in pain.

'Yeah, I know, Tel. I'm a little disappointed too. He used to be the best. Now look at him,' Snipe said, talking to thin air beside him.

As Danny quickly jumped back onto his feet, Snipe sprung nimbly over the ducting before moving towards him, his legs bent, arms up with shoulders relaxed, and hands open. Ignoring the pain, Danny's eyes narrowed and darkened as he did the same. It was a stance he knew well, a stance that would lead to a mixed martial arts form of fighting that both he and Snipe had learned in the SAS. The blows started in perfect sync with each other, their lightning reflexes and heightened reactions causing a stalemate of blocks to each other's blows. The kicks, knees, punches, and elbows got faster and faster, both of them moving rapidly while their heads and eyes remained locked and focused on each other. Danny eventually got through Snipe's blocks with a sharp knee into Snipe's side. He followed it by whipping his elbow up to catch Snipe under the chin, the blow sending him staggering back into the metal ventilation duct.

'That's more like it. Come on, Pearson, give it your best shot,' Snipe said, bringing his head forward as he pushed himself off the ducting.

Seizing the chance, Danny turned and ran for the phone and gun. The sound of Snipe's footsteps hammering on the roof felt close behind him. He grabbed the phone as soon as he reached the air-conditioning unit, stretching across to pick up the gun with his other hand. Snipe rugby tackled him away before he could get his fingers around it. The two men rolled over each other until Danny managed to throw Snipe off and bounce up onto his feet. He frantically stabbed at the phone to get the messages up, flicking his eyes from the screen to Snipe, and then back to the screen again.

'You're too late, me old mate. Time's up. Central London should be crispier than a Peking duck about now,' Snipe said, a wide grin spreading across his face.

'Bastard,' Danny yelled, throwing the phone so it spun end over end, travelling in a blur towards the point between Snipe's eyes.

Snipe flicked his hand up and caught it with barely a glance. He turned it over in his fingers and smiled.

'This is where it all started. The drugs, the tests. We're superhuman, you and me. I've even been dead a few times. Maybe I'm immortal as well. We could have been best mates, if you hadn't been such a self righteous pain in the arse,' Snipe said, tossing the phone over his shoulder before moving in on Danny.

Burning with an inner fury at his friends being burned to a crisp by Snipe's nuclear bomb, Danny moved in to meet him with a blisteringly fast combination of punches to the body and head. The speed of the attack only gave him a momentary advantage before Snipe came back at him, attacking Danny's weaknesses with blows to his injured stomach and shoulder.

For every blow he blocked, Snipe would get another through. He doubled over, his body wracked with pain. Snipe grabbed Danny's hair with both hands, pulling him down as he thrust his knee up into Danny's face. The blow was like being hit with a sledgehammer, his whole body flying backwards to land flat on his back on the roof.

Barely conscious, Danny felt something sharp in his pocket dig into his side. Snipe grabbed Danny's jacket at the front and started dragging him towards the edge of the roof. As his brain tried to make sense of what was happening, he was vaguely aware of the sound of a car skidding to a halt somewhere in the car park below.

'Come over here and watch. This is for you, Tel, watch this fucker's head pop when it hits the ground,' Snipe said, looking behind him at the image of his brother.

Danny looked around, dazed, as Snipe slid him so his head was over the edge of the roof. Turning it to the side, Danny looked down to see David Tremain standing by his car, shouting something up at him. He tried to make out the words as he grabbed Snipe's wrist with his left hand and tried to prise it off of him. Snipe just laughed at his efforts as he prepared to launch Danny off the roof.

'Hold on, Daniel, they defused the bomb. It didn't go off. Help is on the way.'

David's words from below echoed in his head as the fog cleared and clarity of thought returned. He looked up at Snipe to see his face contort with insane rage at the news that they'd defused his bomb. He glared down at Danny, his muscles flexing as he pushed him further over the edge. As his shoulders hung in midair, Danny punched his right hand into Snipe's chest. There was a surprised look on Snipe's face as Danny pulled back and punched him again and again. Snipe's grip loosened on Danny as he dropped to his knees, spraying out blood as he coughed. As Danny pulled his hand back, the five-inch-long boning knife he'd taken from the kitchen to cut David loose glinted in the lights from the car park. Snipe looked down at Danny and across at his brother.

He whispered 'Terry?' before toppling silently off the roof.

Danny rolled safely back onto the surface of the roof, sucking in great gulps of air.

'Daniel, are you alright?' David's shouts came from below.

Barely able to answer, Danny swung his arm over the edge and gave a thumbs up. When he was able, he dragged himself upright and picked his gun up off the air-conditioning unit, then made his way slowly downstairs.

David was kneeling beside Snipe in the long grass between the building and the car park when Danny got outside.

'Good god, you look like hell,' David said, turning his head and then turning it back to Snipe. 'Christ, I've got a pulse. He's still alive.'

David jumped at the sound of gunfire as Danny put two bullets into Snipe's head. Blood, bone, and bits of brain stained the grass as the exiting bullets ripped the back of his skull out.

'You'll bloody well stay dead this time,' he muttered, limping towards his car. 'This is your mess. You can clear it up. I'm going home,' Danny said over his shoulder.

David didn't argue with him. He watched him spin the car around in the car park and power it away down the drive. No more than five minutes later, a helicopter carrying a special forces tactical team thundered in low over the trees and landed in the car park while David stood waiting for them.

CHAPTER 66

'Remember, play it down. It looks worse than it is, ok?' Danny said to Scott.

'Of course, dear boy, although I'm not sure how it could look much worse,' Scott replied with a chuckle.

'That's not helping, Scott. I promised Nikki this wouldn't happen again, and now look at me.'

Scott did look at him, with his arm back in a sling, healing cuts and bruises across his knuckles, and the remnants of blackish-blue bruising around his eyes.

'Here, wear these. It'll be fine, just let me do all the talking,' said Scott with his usual air of confidence as he handed Danny his sunglasses.

'What's wrong with these? I can't see a bloody thing,' Danny said, trying to make out the fuzzy writing of the airport arrivals board.

'They're my prescription pair, and it's probably a good thing, because here she comes and she's not looking too happy,' Scott said, seeing his sister enter the arrivals hall, smiling excitedly until she saw the state of Danny looking sheepish as he stood behind Scott.

'What the hell's happened now?' she said, trying to move around Scott.

'Now hang on, sis, it really wasn't his fault. This hulking, great psychopath from Daniel's past came back from the dead and tried to kill him. He was lucky really, the brute killed a dozen people before coming after him, and he tried to blow up London with a nuclear bomb. What are the odds? You couldn't make it up,' Scott said, in a cheery, upbeat fashion.

'Really, Scott! That's your idea of helping,' Danny said, sliding off Scott's sunglasses and handing them back to him as he stepped past to greet Nikki.

'Sorry, old man, I got a bit carried away,' Scott said in a huff.

'Is this sort of thing ever going to stop happening to you?' Nikki said, her face changing from cross to concerned as she hugged him tight.

'Argh, ouch, easy does it,' he winced while trying to decide which part of him hurt the most.

'I love you,' she finally said, pulling her face away from his chest to kiss him.

'I love you too,' he said, smiling, then wincing again as his healing lip cracked its scab.

'You see, I was of some use,' said Scott, beaming.

'Shut up, you idiot,' both Nikki and Danny said at the same time.

'Charming,' Scott replied.

After Scott dropped them off at Danny's, he left them to settle in. Danny made them both a brew and fell more than sat painfully into the sofa. Nikki joined him, curling up close.

'So the house sale is all going through then?' Danny asked.

'Yes, I've cleared it out and shipped some of my personal things here. The estate agents are dealing with everything else, so I don't need to go back.'

'So, you still want to marry me then?' Danny said, a little unsure of himself after recent events.

'Of course I do. All this is who you are, and I love you, as you are,' Nikki said, giving him a warm smile.

'Phew, that's lucky, because the boys have been hounding me about a stag weekend in Benidorm.'

'Oi, is that all you're worried about?' said Nikki, poking him in the ribs so it hurt.

'No, of course not. I just want you.'

'That's the right answer, Mr Pearson. There is one thing I want you to do for me,' she said, turning to face him.

'What's that?'

'I want you to teach me.'

'Teach you what?' Danny said, puzzled.

'After Australia, that thing in Colombia, and now this. I want you to teach me everything—how to fight and shoot, how to look after myself and keep us safe in case this ever happens again.'

Danny looked her in the eye. He could tell she was deadly serious.

'Ok I'll teach you,' he finally said.

CHAPTER 67

D r Wallace drove up to the barrier and lowered his window to flash his ID card at the same military police officer he did every day of the week. As usual, the futility of it crossed his mind the way it did every day of the week; they knew who he was so why did he need to show the ID? He smiled and drove into the car park of the MoD facility, and parked in his usual spot. Grabbing the Costa coffee from the cup holder and his leather briefcase, he headed inside.

'Morning, Doctor,' the two men on security said in unison, one sitting behind the x-ray machine as the doctor placed his leather briefcase on the conveyor belt, the way he did every morning. The other waved for him to walk through the metal detector.

'Have a good day,' he said as the doctor swigged his coffee and picked up his case.

'Thank you, Bruce, and you.'

He walked through the facility, tapping his pass card on the multitude of locks, until he reached the locker room, where he finished his coffee and put on his lab coat. Another tap of the card later, and he entered the lab itself.

'Morning, Dr Wallace, how are you this morning?'

'Very well, Alisha, er, have you got the DNA results back from subject 894 yet?'

'Oh yes, Doctor, they're on your desk. They have some of the same unusual genetic markers as test subject 895.'

'Really, interesting. Could you fetch me tissue samples of each subject from the cryo room? I'd like to run some more cell tests.'

'Certainly, Doctor,' Alisha replied, heading off to the cryogenic sample storage room.

The doctor entered his office and opened the folder with the DNA results. He studied them, then pulled the file for subject 895. He held them side by side while he waited for his computer to boot up, then opened his email program and typed.

"Dear General, we have had a breakthrough on the samples from test subject 894, Nicholas Snipe, and test subject 895, Daniel Pearson. The identification and duplication of the enhanced DNA markers has been successful. I feel we are now in a position to proceed with the Genome Editing Program on live test subjects."

He hit send and sat back, his mind racing with the possibilities. Seeing Alisha return with the tissue samples through his office window, he shut the files and slid them back into the cabinet before walking through.

'Ok, here we go, another day, another sample test,' he joked, the same joke he did every morning.

ABOUT THE AUTHOR

Stephen Taylor is a successful British Thriller writer. His Amazon bestselling Danny Pearson series has sold well over 150,000 copies, and delighted lovers of the action and adventure thriller genre. Before becoming a novelist, he ran his own business, installing audio visual equipment for homes and businesses.

With the big 50 approaching, Stephen wrote the book he'd always wanted to. That book was Execution Of Faith. A supercharged, action packed roller coaster of a ride that doesn't take itself too seriously. People loved the book so much he wrote a prequel Vodka Over London Ice. Because of the timeline, this became the first in the Danny Pearson Thriller Series

Born out of his love of action thriller books, Lee Child's Jack Reacher, Vince Flynn's Mitch Rapp and Tom Wood's Victor. Not to mention his love of action movies, Die Hard, Daniel Craig's Bond and Guy Richie's Lock Stock or Snatch. The Danny Pearson series moves along with hard and fast action, no filler, and a healthy dose of humour to move it along.